The
Further Adventures
of Slugger McBatt

The Further Adventures of Slugger McBatt

Baseball Stories by W. P. Kinsella

COLLINS • TORONTO

First published in Canada 1988
by Collins Publishers
100 Lesmill Road, Don Mills, Ontario

Canadian Cataloguing in Publication Data

Kinsella, W.P.
 The further adventures of Slugger McBatt

1st paperback ed.
ISBN 0-00-223281-2

I. Title.

PS8571.I57F87 1988a   C813'.54   C88-093407-7
PR9199.3.K59F87 1988a

Some of the stories in this collection have appeared elsewhere, in slightly different form: "Distances" in *Sport Magazine*; "Reports Concerning the Death of the Seattle Albatross Are Somewhat Exaggerated" in *The Seattle Review*; "Frank Pierce, Iowa" in *Five Stories*, a chapbook published by William Hoffer of Vancouver, British Columbia; "K Mart" in *Arete: Journal of Sports Literature*; "Diehard" in *Spitball: The Literary Baseball Magazine* and *Five Stories*; and "Searching for Freddy" in *Canadian Fiction Magazine*.

Printed and bound in the United States of America

For Memo Luna
on his induction into the Mexican Baseball Hall of Fame.

For my fellow owners
in the Sixties Lezcano Ultimate Baseball Association:
Mike Carroll, Kevin Cremin, Commissioner Jack
(Don Guido) Fleming, J. Michael Kenyon, Ann Knight,
Rick Rizzs, and Bob Rosenweig.

CONTENTS

Distances

THE CADILLAC was the color of thick, rich cream. It pulled up in front of Mrs. Richards's Springtime Café and Ice Cream Parlor. The main street of Onamata was paved, but the pavement was narrow; there was six feet of gravel between the edge of the pavement and the wooden sidewalk. Dust from the gravel whooshed past the car and oozed through the screen door of the café.

My friend Stan Rogalski and I were seated at a tile table, our feet hooked on the insect-legged chairs. We were sharing a dish of vanilla ice cream, savoring each bite, trying to make it outlast the heat of high July.

It was easy to tell the Cadillac owner was a man who cared about his car. He checked his rearview carefully before opening the driver's door. After he got out, or *unwound* would be a better description, for he was six foot five if he was an inch, he closed the door gently but firmly, then wiped something off the sideview mirror. On the way around the Caddy he picked something off the grille and flicked it onto the road.

He took a seat in a corner of the café where he could watch his car and everyone else in the café, which at the moment was me, Stan, and Mrs. Richards. My name is Gideon Clarke.

The stranger looked to be in his mid-thirties; he had rusty hair combed into a high pompadour that accentuated his tall front teeth and made his face look longer than it really was. Across his upper lip was a wide mustache with the corners turned up; the mustache was the same coppery red as the hair on his head. I guessed he'd worn his hair in a spiffy duck-ass cut in the fifties, but now the duck ass was out of style. Elvis was being replaced by Chubby Checker, and it would be a long time before long hair was in fashion in the Midwest. The stranger's hair was combed back at the sides, hiding the top half of his ears. At the back, it covered his collar and turned up a little at the ends.

"I'd like something tall and cool," he said when Mrs. Richards waddled over to his table.

"I have pink lemonade," she said in a tiny voice that belied her 250 pounds.

"I'll have the biggest size you've got," he said.

After Mrs. Richards delivered the lemonade in a sweaty, opaque glass, he took a long drink, stretched his legs, and looked around the room. He was wearing a black suit with fine gray pinstripes, a white-on-white shirt, and shoes that must have cost fifty dollars.

"What do you figure he does?" whispered Stan. When I didn't answer quickly he went on. "A banker, I bet, or an undertaker, maybe."

"He's suntanned," I said. "And look at his hands." The knuckles were scarred, the fingers calloused.

"What then?"

"Howdy, boys," the stranger said, and raised his glass to us. His voice was deep and soft.

"Hi," we said.

"I see you're ballplayers," he said, nodding toward our gloves, which rested on the floor by the chair legs. "Is there much baseball played in these parts?"

The question was like opening a floodgate. Stan and I told him about everything from the Little League to the Onamata High School team we played for to the University of Iowa ball club to the commercial leagues that had teams in Iowa City, Onamata, Lone Tree, West Branch, and other nearby towns.

"How did your team do this year?" he asked us, not in the way most adults have of patronizing young people, but with genuine interest.

"Well," I said, "we were two and nineteen for the season. But we're really a lot better ball club than that," I rushed on before he could interrupt. The stranger didn't laugh as most adults would have. "I kept statistics. We scored more runs than any team in the league. We're good hitters, average fielders, but we didn't have anyone who could pitch. A bad team gets beat seventeen to two. We would get beat seventeen to fourteen, nineteen to twelve, eighteen to sixteen. We're really good hitters, especially Stan here. Stan's gonna make it to the Bigs."

"I practice three hours a day, all year round," said Stan, picking up my enthusiasm. "In winter I throw in the loft of our barn."

"Then you'll probably make it," said the stranger.

"You look like you might be a player yourself," I said.

"I've pitched a few innings in my day," he said with what I recognized as understatement, and he rose from his chair and made his way, with two long strides, to our table.

"The thought struck me that you boys might like another dish of ice cream."

"You've had a good thought," said Stan.

"I notice my lemonade cost twenty-five cents, as does a dish of ice cream. I might be willing to make a small wager."

"What kind?" we both said, staring up at him.

"Well now, I'm willing to bet I can tell you the exact distance in miles between any two major American cities."

"How far is it from Iowa City to Davenport?" said Stan quickly.

"Those are not major American cities," said the stranger, "but I noticed as I was driving in that the distance was sixty-two miles. What I had in mind, though, were large cities. Des Moines would qualify, as would Kansas City, New Orleans, Los Angeles, Seattle, Dallas."

"How far from New York to Chicago?" said Stan.

"Exactly 809 miles," said the stranger.

"How do we know you're not making that up?" I said.

"A good question," said the stranger. "Out in my car I have a road atlas and inside it is a United States mileage chart. If one of you boys would like to get it for me . . ." As he spoke he reached a large hand into a side pocket and withdrew his keys. I grabbed them and was halfway across the room before Stan could untangle his feet from the chair legs.

The interior of the car was still cool from the air conditioning. It smelled of leather and lime aftershave. There was nothing in sight except a State Farm road atlas on the white leather of the front seat. The very neatness of the car told a lot about its owner, I thought: neat, methodical, the type of man who would care about distances.

I carried the atlas into the café, where the stranger was now seated across the table from Stan.

"Let's just check out New York to Chicago," he said. "There's always a chance I could be wrong."

He turned to the United States Mileage Chart, and all three of us studied it for a moment. In groups of five, in alphabetical order, there were eighty cities listed down the side of the chart; sixty names were across the top. Where the two names intersected was the mileage between them.

"Yes, sir, 809 miles, just as I said." The stranger put a big, square finger tip down on the chart at the point where New York and Chicago intersected.

Up close, I noticed the stranger had a lantern jaw. He was also more muscular than I would have guessed, his shoulders square as a robot's. His eyes were golden.

I quickly calculated that there were nearly five thousand squares on the mileage chart. He can't know them all, I thought.

"Would either of you care to test me?" he asked, smiling. "By the way, my name's Roger Cash."

"Gideon Clarke," I said. "My friend, Stan Rogalski."

We both had money in our pockets, but we were saving for a trip to Chicago. My father had promised to take us up for an entire Cubs home stand.

"Well . . ."

"No bets, then. Just name some places. Distances are my hobby."

"Omaha and New Orleans," I said.

"1026," Roger Cash replied, after an appropriate pause.

We checked it and he was right.

"St. Louis to Los Angeles," said Stan.

"Exactly 1836 miles," said Roger.

Again he was right.

"Milwaukee to Kansas City," I said.

"1779," he replied quickly.

We checked the chart.

"Wrong!" we chorused together. "It's 1797."

"Doggone, I tend to reverse numbers sometimes," he said with a grin. "Seeing as how I couldn't do it three times in a row, I'll buy you men a dish of ice cream each, or something larger if you want. A banana split? You choose."

It wasn't often we could afford top-of-the-line treats. I ordered a banana split with chopped almonds and chocolate sauce on all three scoops of ice cream. Stan ordered a tall chocolate malt, thick as cement. Roger had another lemonade.

"What made you memorize the mileage chart?" I asked between mouthfuls.

"Nothing made me," said Roger, leaning back and stretching out his legs. "I spend a lot of time traveling, a lot of nights alone in hotel rooms. It passes the time, beats drinking or reading the Gideon Bible. No offense," he then said to me. "I don't suppose that book's named after you anyway."

"No, sir, I reckon it wasn't."

"I've been known to gamble," he went on, "on my ability to remember mileages, on the outcome of baseball games in which I am the pitcher. Never gamble unless the odds are on your side."

"Do you pitch for anyone in particular?" I asked.

"I tried to take a team barnstorming one season. Unfortunately that era is long gone. I used to watch the House of David and the Kansas City Monarchs on tour when I was a kid. Costs too much to support a traveling team these days, and television has killed attendance at minor-league parks. No, what I do now is arrange for a pickup team to back me up — play an exhibition game against a well-known local team . . . . Say . . ." he said, and paused as if he had just been struck by a brilliant idea. "Do you suppose you men could round up the rest of your high school team? What did you say the name of this town is?"

"Onamata," we said together. "And sure, most of the players live on farms around here. We could round up a full team with no trouble at all."

"Well, in that case I think we might be able to arrange a business proposition," he said.

For the next few minutes, while Roger Cash outlined his plans, Stan and I nodded at his every suggestion. It was obvious he had done this kind of thing many times before.

All the time he was talking I had been eyeing the mileage chart, searching for an easily reversible number.

"Have you spotted one that will beat me?" Roger said suddenly.

"Maybe."

"You want to put some money on it?"

"A dollar," I said, and gulped; I could feel the pace of my heart pick up.

"Yer on," he said, turning his head away from where the chart lay open on the tabletop. "Name the cities."

"Albuquerque to New York."

Roger laughed. "You picked one of the hardest. A mileage easy to reverse. Now if I wanted to win your dollar I'd say '1997'." He paused for one beat. I could feel my own heart bump, for the number he gave was right. "But if I wanted to set you up to bet five dollars on the next combination, I'd say '1979.' I might miss the next one, too. People are greedy and they like to take money from a stranger. I might even miss a third or fourth time, and I always leave the chart out where a man with a sharp eye can spot another easily reversible number. You men aren't old enough to go in bars, or I'd show you how it works in actual practice."

I took out my wallet and lifted out a dollar.

"No," said Roger. "Experience. I'll chalk that dollar up to *your* experience. I have a mind for distances. I once read a story about a blind, retarded boy who played the piano like a master. And I heard about another man who can tell you what day of the week any date in history, or future history, was or will be. I have an idiot's talent for distances."

"What's so great about distances?" said Stan. "I think if I was smart I'd choose something else to be an expert on."

"Let me tell you about distances," said Roger, his golden eyes like coins with black shadows at the center. "Six or eight inches doesn't make any difference if the distance is, say, between Des Moines and Los Angeles, right?"

We nodded in agreement.

"Now suppose you're in bed with your girlfriend." He moved forward, hunching over the table, lowering his voice, because over behind the counter Mrs. Richards was doing her best to hear all of our conversation. "Suppose your peter won't do what it's supposed to do. If it won't produce that six or eight inches, no matter how close you are to pussy, you might as well be 1709 miles away, which is how far it is from Des Moines to Los Angeles." We all sat back and laughed. At the counter Mrs. Richards smiled crossly.

"The distances in baseball are perfect," Roger went on, "ninety feet from base to base, sixty feet six inches from the mound to the plate. Not too far, not too close. Change any one of them six or eight inches, the length of your peter, and the whole game would be out of kilter."

We nodded, wide-eyed.

"Well, since we've got a team, all we have to do is find ourselves an opponent," said Roger. "Here's what I have in mind. Who's the best pitcher in these parts?"

"That would be Silas Erb," I said. "Chucks for Procter and Gamble in the Division One Commercial League."

"Is he crafty or a hardball thrower?"

"Ninety miles an hour straight down the middle, dares anybody to hit it."

"Scratch him. I want a guy who's a curve baller, maybe tries to throw a screwball, has a wicked change."

"That'd be McCracken. McCracken Construction have been Division One champs two years in a row."

"And he owns the company?"

"His daddy does."

"Would he be the kind to accept a challenge from an elderly baseball pitcher with a two-and-nineteen high school team on the field in back of him?"

"Who wouldn't?"

"If we were to get posters printed and build up this challenge game, what sort of attendance do you men think we could expect here in Onamata?"

"People are hungry for baseball," I said. "The King and His Court fast-ball team drew over a thousand in Iowa City in June. I think we could get five or six hundred out to Onamata for a game like that."

"At three dollars a head?"

"Sounds fair."

Roger Cash grinned, the right side of his mouth opening up to show his dice-like teeth. I noticed then, even while he had a suit on, that his right bicep was huge, many inches larger than the left one.

"Would you men care to accompany me into Iowa City this evening? You could point out Mr. McCracken's residence to me. We'll discuss our financial situation at the same time."

What he proposed to McCracken that night was a winner-take-all game, the Onamata High School team with Roger Cash pitching against McCracken Construction, Division One Champs and one of the best commercial league teams in the state.

" 'And of course,' I said to him," Cash told us later, " 'I'll be happy to cover any wagers you, your teammates, or the good citizens of

Iowa City or Onamata might like to make, all in strictest confidence of course.'

"'At what odds?' McCracken said to me.

"'Even odds, of course,' I said. 'Roger Cash is not greedy.' And you should have seen him smile.

"'I'd like to see you work out,' McCracken said to me.

"'Oh no,' I said. 'The element of surprise is all I've got on my side. I hear tell you played in Triple A for a year, so it's not likely anything an old pitcher like me can throw will surprise you. Myself, I played a dozen games one summer for a Class C team in Greensboro, North Carolina, but they didn't pay me enough to keep my mustache waxed so I moved on. Actually they suggested I move on, but that's another story.' I smiled real friendly at him."

Back in Onamata, after the game was set, Roger led us to the trunk of his car. As he opened the trunk of the cream-colored Caddy, Stan and I were on our tiptoes, staring over and around him. The trunk was almost as austere as the car interior. It contained a black valise, very old, almost triangular, with heavy brass latches, and a canvas duffel bag with a pair of worn black baseball cleats tied around the drawstring at its neck. A few garden tools were cast diagonally in the trunk: a rake, a hoe, a small spoon-nosed shovel. There was no spare wheel, and built into the depression where the wheel would ordinarily have been was what looked like a small, black safe, anchored in concrete in the wheel well. There was no dirt or dust, nothing extraneous.

"We're going to need some money to finance the operation," he said, and smiled slowly, lines appearing in the deeply tanned skin around his eyes. "I'll have to ask you gentlemen to turn your backs while I operate on Black Betsy here. I'd also be obliged if you kept the secret of her existence among the three of us."

The final statement was a command, though it wasn't worded like one. Stan and I busied ourselves staring up and down the street and studying the front of the Springtime Café while Roger Cash turned the dial on the safe. It made sounds like a bicycle lock.

"You can turn around now," he said.

The safe was stuffed with money. I have no idea how much, though I did see that most of the bills were hundreds.

The deal was that each of the eight players to back him up were to get twenty dollars for the game. Stan and I got more for distributing 250 posters to businesses in downtown Iowa City and Onamata. We also distributed a thousand handbills to homes, as well as placing them on car windshields. And we were to be paid for selling tickets right up until game time. Roger suggested that we arrange to sell hot dogs, soda, and popcorn, since no one ever bothered to do that at the Onamata Baseball Grounds. He even peeled off a few bills from a collar-sized roll he carried, advancing us enough to buy and rent what supplies we needed, as well as to hire people for the concessions. In return, we were to split the profits. In the next few days Stan and I felt like real businessmen, going around hiring women three times our age to work for us the next Sunday.

Roger needed a place to stay. There was no hotel in Onamata, never had been. I was quick to volunteer our home, where my father and I lived alone in an elegant old frame house with a wrought-iron widow's walk. My father was engaged in a peculiar baseball research project, which took up most of his time. He left the operation of Clarke and Son Insurance to his secretary.

"I need to ask you for another favor," Roger said the next morning. "I need a place to work out, a private place. An old dog like me has to have surprise on his side. I don't want McCracken or any of his spies to see me pitch until game time."

"I think I can arrange that," I said. "My friends have a farm a mile from town. Mr. and Mrs. Baron are like grandparents to me. I know we can set up in their pasture."

A quick trip to Barons' and we were able to find a natural pitcher's mound in the pasture below the house. A few minutes with the tools from Roger's trunk, and we imbedded a length of two-by-four in the mound. We dug a small depression and inset two pieces of wood side by side to form a crude plate after Roger had produced a well-worn tape from his duffel bag and measured out the exact distance from home to the pitcher's mound. I held the beginning of the tape on the mound while he measured to the spot where home plate should be.

Roger then dug out his glove and a ball. He gave me the glove and threw a few practice pitches while I crouched behind the newly installed plate. I guess I was expecting Sandy Koufax, because after about fifteen pitches I said, with that terrible candor the young consider honesty, "You're not very good."

"You haven't seen me with an enemy batter at the plate," he replied. "I may not look like much, and I'm no Juan Marichal, but I change speeds, keep the hitters off balance; keeping hitters off balance is a pitcher's most important function."

Since the game was set for the following Sunday afternoon, the preparations kept Stan and I running all week. Tuesday night we scouted McCracken Construction during a league game in Iowa City. McCracken pitched; he was a stocky, barrel-chested man with blue-black hair. He pitched a three-hitter. Roger made notes on the batters he would have to face.

After the game we discussed strategy.

"I'm gonna have you lead off," Roger said to me. I had kept statistics on our team's whole season, and I showed them to Roger. Stan kept track of only his own batting average; I took home scorecards after each game and calculated everyone's batting average, on-base percentage, and fielding average.

"I'm slow on the bases," I said. "I never honestly stole a base all season."

"You get on, though," he said. "You hit singles, and more importantly, you walk. Walks are very important. You need patience to walk. I'm going to put my batters up in the order of their patience."

"I don't understand," I said. "McCracken has great control."

"It's a strategy," said Roger, as he smiled disarmingly.

We had one practice Friday evening. I'm afraid we didn't look very good. Someone from McCracken's team sat in a pickup truck about three blocks down the street, studying us through binoculars.

Roger did not pitch. Our regular pitcher, Dusty Swan, threw batting practice.

"I want you guys to lay back and wait for the fast ball," Roger told us. "McCracken's got a killer curve, a mean slider, a big-league change-up you can break your back on, but his fast ball's nothing; he uses it to set up his other pitches. If we can keep from swinging at anything outside the strike zone, he'll give up lots of walks. Then he'll have to throw the fast ball, and when he does we'll hammer it."

All that week Roger worked out at Barons' in the afternoons, but at night he played the mileage game in every bar in Iowa City. According to the stories we heard, he picked up several hundred dollars each night. It was also a way for Roger to become known quickly, assuring a good crowd at the ball game on Sunday. At the end of his third day in town he had a very pretty coed from the University of Iowa on his arm. Her name was Jacqueline, and she spent the rest of the nights that week in Roger's room, except the night before the big game.

"Do you have any objection, Mr. Clarke," Roger said to my father our first night at supper together, "to my having occasional female company in my room?"

My father looked up from the page of statistics he was studying as he ate, stared at Roger, blinking, perhaps trying to remember who he was.

"Oh no," he said, smiling almost shyly. "You can bring a goat to your room as far as I'm concerned, as long as you're quiet."

It was during that same week that I found out a lot about distances myself. Most of my friends had not discovered girls yet. Oh, we talked about them individually and collectively, usually in a disparaging manner, repeating gossip we heard from older boys at the café or the pool hall. Stan went to the movies in Iowa City a few times with a pale blonde girl named Janice, who wore no lipstick or make-up because her family belonged to some fanatical religious splinter group that thought the end of the world imminent, and taught that we all should be in a natural state when the end came.

"I asked her why she wore clothes," said Stan, after his third and final date. The only reason her parents let her go out with Stan was that he appeared to be a likely candidate for conversion.

The third evening, when they arrived back at her house after the show (her father drove them to the theater and picked them up at the Hamburg Inn afterward), their preacher, a Pastor Valentine, and eight members of the congregation were camped in the living room, which Stan said was decorated like a church interior. Pastor Valentine conducted a service where everyone prayed loud and long for Stan's wandering soul. They said many unkind things about the Catholic Church in general and the Pope in particular, having assumed wrongly that Stan was a practicing Roman Catholic. Stan's family were actually lapsed Catholics with no church affiliation.

That summer I was in love for the first time. Her name was Julie Dornhoffer, and I had become enamored of her just at the end of the school year. She was a robust farm girl, almost my height, and a good fifteen pounds heavier. But she had a healthy quality about her and she always looked me in the eye when we talked. She sometimes drove a four-ton grain truck to school. I liked her straightforwardness, her toughness. I have always been repelled by delicate girls in pastels and cosmetics. Julie tolerated my interest, but made it clear she would prefer a more masculine beau. She teased me about my ignorance of farms and was slightly contemptuous of my physical strength. Also, I didn't drive yet. Julie had been driving farm equipment since she was ten.

I called on her about once a week, walking the three miles of un-paved road to the farm. She would entertain me in the dark parlor of the house, or we would walk in the sweet dusk, watching fireflies rising, sparkling, dissolving in our path. We even kissed a few times. But I knew my interest in her was much greater than her interest in me.

A couple of days after Roger Cash arrived in town, I walked out to the Dornhoffer farm. I arrived at midafternoon on a high-skied, blazing day. The farmhouse was tall and sad-looking, badly in need of paint. I knocked at the side door, and a large woman whom I recognized as one of Julie's aunts answered, wiping perspiration from her forehead with the back of her hand.

"Julie and her sister're coiling hay back in the north pasture," she said. I could not see into the house because of the thick screen on the door, but from the dark interior came the smell of pork roast, the fumes mouth-watering, almost tangible.

I walked through a grove of trees, enjoying the coolness in the midst of the fiery day. I picked a bluebell or two, split the bell, and rooted out the teardrop of honey inside the flower.

On the other side of the trees was a small field of red clover. Half of it had recently been swathed. Julie and a younger sister were at work with pitchforks, layering the hay into coils, which when finished resembled giant beehives.

"You townies don't know how good you've got it," Julie said, driving the tines into the earth, stilling the vibrating fork handle, then leaning on it as if it were a tree. She was flushed and perspiring. Her copper-colored hair spilled over her forehead and was flecked with clover seeds. She wore jeans and a short-sleeved blouse the color of wild roses. The back and underarms of the blouse were soaked dark. She wasn't wearing a bra. I realized that even after my three-mile walk I was still cool. I was wearing a white, open-necked shirt and khaki shorts. My own hair was white as vanilla ice cream, and I was hardly tanned at all. Julie's arms and face were sun-blackened, her hair bleached golden in spots.

"Can I help?" I said, hoping somehow to win her favor.

"Sure," she said, smiling too knowingly, as if there was some private joke I was not in on. "Beat it," she said to her sister, and the younger girl stabbed her fork into the ground and raced off, happy to be relieved of an unpleasant job.

I have probably never worked as hard as I did in the next fifteen minutes and accomplished less. I might as well have been trying to coil water with that pitchfork. I babbled on about my friend Roger Cash, the upcoming baseball game, mileages, distances, posters, concessions, all the while accumulating a pitiful pile of clover in front of me. No matter what I did to it, it had no resemblance to the waist-high beehives Julie and her sister had created; in each coil they had made the hay was swirled, the swaths interlocked, impervious to wind, resistant to rain.

While I worked and talked Julie relaxed, sitting back in the shade of a green coil, smoking, a crockery water jug bathed in condensation beside her.

I finally gave up and joined her, red-faced and disheveled.

"It's not as easy as it looks," I said.

Julie grinned with what I hoped was tolerance rather than contempt.

"You people in town live so far away," she said, her tone still not definable.

"It's only three miles," I said stupidly.

Julie crushed out her cigarette in the earth beside her. She looked at me with a close-lipped smile. "At least you tried," she said, and leaned over so her head rested on my shoulder.

We kissed, both our faces damp from the heat of the day. The smell of freshly cut clover was overpowering. Julie slid closer to me, crossed one of my bare legs with her denim one. She radiated heat. Her breasts burned against my chest, only two thin layers of cloth separating us. Her tongue was deep in my mouth, her large right hand gripped hard on my left shoulder. She was forcing me down onto my back, pushing me deep into the sweet clover. I didn't mind that she was stronger than I was; there was nothing I could do about that; it even excited me. I ran my free hand down the thigh of her jeans, let it find its way between her legs.

We stopped kissing and gasped for breath.

"I bet I could take you," Julie said into my neck, and I knew by her tone that she meant in physical strength.

"You probably could," I said, sitting up, gasping for air. "What does it matter? You work hard, I don't — " But she forced me back down, my head going deep into the hay. All the sexuality of the moment was gone. This was a contest. Julie's hands were on my shoulders. Her right leg was between my thighs; she held my back down flat on the stubbly earth.

I had no experience roughhousing with girls. My own sister, a year older than me, had always been a deadly serious child, resentful and threatening, someone I avoided physical contact with.

My worst fear, a fear I was almost certain was a truth, was that

Julie would *care* about being able to outwrestle me. How hard should I defend myself? I'd taken a few wrestling lessons in physical education class. If I was to concentrate on one of her arms, get a solid lock on it . . . But I was flat on my back with Julie sitting on my chest. My shoulders were pinned to the earth, my head partially covered with clover, which choked my senses, the tiny red seeds filling my eyes and mouth, spilling down my neck.

I bucked ineffectually a few times.

"Okay, you've proved your point," I said.

Julie threw herself to one side and scrambled to her feet. I stood and brushed the clover seeds from my face and shirt front. I smiled at Julie, hoping to make a joke of my defeat. But what I read in her eyes said that I was never to be forgiven for my weakness. I was walking toward her with the idea of taking her in my arms, in spite of the coldness in her eyes, when her sister reappeared.

"We've got to get back to work," said Julie, dismissing me.

"I'll see you again," I said. Julie didn't reply.

As I walked slowly back toward Onamata, I knew I would never call on her again.

Saturday night, Roger went to bed about ten o'clock.

"Got to rest the old soupbone," he said, flexing his pitching arm, which was muscular and huge, as he headed up the stairs.

I went to bed shortly after him, but I couldn't sleep. My mind was too full of the game the next day; my thoughts were as much on the operation of the concessions as on baseball itself. I eventually dozed fitfully. Late in the night I woke with a start, surprised to hear the stairs creaking. I stretched out my arm and let the rays of moonlight slanting through the window touch the face of my watch. It was three A.M. I went to the window. I heard Roger's keys jingle in the darkness, watched as he opened the trunk to the Caddy and stealthily extracted the garden tools, hoisted them to his shoulder, and set off down the fragrant, moonstruck street.

About four-fifteen, just as the first tines of pink appeared on the horizon, Roger returned, replaced the gardening tools, and re-entered the house.

By game time we had sold 511 tickets; I left Margie Smood at the ticket table to sell to latecomers until the fifth inning. The concessions were booming, and the air was riddled with the smell of frying onions, hot dogs, and popcorn. There was no fence around the ballfield. At Roger's suggestion, we constructed a funnel-like gate with pickets joined by flaming orange plastic ribbons. People were generally honest; only a few school kids and a handful of adults skirted the ticket line.

We were all nervous as we warmed up along the first-base side. One thing we forgot to tell Roger was that Onamata High had never been able to afford uniforms, so we wore whatever each of us could scrounge, from jeans, T-shirts, and sneakers to a full Detroit Tiger uniform worn by Lindy Dean, who was a cousin a couple of times removed from Dizzy Trout.

Across the way, McCracken Construction, in black uniforms with gold numbers on their chests and their names in gold letters on their backs, snapped balls back and forth with authority. Baseballs smacking into gloves sounded like balloons breaking.

"Where are the gate receipts?" Roger asked me.

"In a box under the ticket table. You don't need to worry. Margie Smood's honest."

"Go get them. Just leave her enough to change a twenty."

"But —"

"I've got to get down some more bets."

"What if we lose?"

"Never in doubt, Gideon. Never in doubt."

I brought him the money, and while the Onamata High School Music Makers Marching Band, all six of them, were assassinating the national anthem, Roger carried the money around behind the backstop, and held a conference with McCracken and his teammates.

The president of the University of Iowa was seated in the front row and he had apparently agreed to hold the bets. By the time the game started there were bags and boxes, envelopes and cartons, piled at his feet. As near as I could guess, Roger had about ten thousand dollars riding on the game, most of it covered by McCracken and members of his team.

Roger and McCracken continued to talk animatedly for several minutes. It was a long discussion, and finally McCracken went to his equipment bag and counted out more money; he also signed something. Roger dug into the back pocket of his uniform and produced the keys to his Caddy. He held them up and let the sun play on them for an instant, then dropped them in a box with the money and notes, which a bat boy carried over and deposited at the feet of the university president.

I noticed that McCracken seemed uncomfortable as he warmed up on the mound. One of the concessions Roger offered right off the top was, even though we were playing in Onamata, to allow McCracken Construction to be home team. I was right about McCracken being uncomfortable; he pawed the dirt and stalked around kicking at the rubber. The first three pitches he threw were low, one bouncing right on the plate. He threw the fast ball then, right down the heart of the plate for a strike. I was tempted to hammer it, but I held back, telling myself, a walk is as good as a single. McCracken was in trouble, I wasn't. He walked me with another low pitch. He walked Lindy Dean on five pitches. He walked Gussy Pulvermacher on four. As I moved to third, I watched Roger whispering in Stan's ear, a heavy arm around his shoulders.

The first pitch was low. The second broke into the dirt. McCracken kicked furiously at the mound. I could almost see Stan's confidence building as he waited. The fast ball came. He drove it into the gap in left-center. Stan had a standup double. Three of us scored in front of him, as Roger, leaping wildly in the third-base coach's box, waved us in.

McCracken was rattled now. It didn't help him that the crowd were mainly for us. Here was a high school team with a 2–19 season record going against a crack amateur team who were state champions two years before, and finalists the last year.

Our next batter walked on four pitches. Then McCracken settled down to his fast ball and struck out the sixth and seventh batters. Our catcher, Walt Swan, hammered the first pitch he got, about five hundred feet to deep left, nearly to the Iowa River. Fortunately for

McCracken, the ball was foul. He reverted to his off-speed pitches and walked Swan.

Roger Cash stepped into the batter's box. He had confided to me that if he had kept a record, his lifetime hitting average would be below .100. But I have to admit he looked formidable in his snow-white uniform with CASH in maroon letters across his shoulders and the large numbers oo in the middle of his back. The front of his uniform had only crossed baseball bats on it. He held the bat straight up and down and waggled it purposefully.

"Throw your fast ball and I'll put it in the river," yelled Roger, and curled his lip at McCracken.

The first pitch was a curve in the dirt, followed by a change-up low, another curve at the ankles, and something that may have been a screwball, that hit two feet in front of the plate. Roger trotted to first. Stan loped home with our fourth run. The bases were still loaded.

On the first pitch McCracken came right down the middle at me with his fast ball. I swung and got part of it on the end of the bat; a dying quail of a single just beyond the second baseman's reach. Runs five and six scored. Lindy Dean ended the inning.

McCracken's team tried to get all six runs back in the first. They went out one-two-three.

In right field, I trembled. My judgment of fly balls was not sound, and the opponents would soon find out that when any ball was hit to me the base runners could do as they pleased. Not only could I not cut a runner down at third, I had trouble getting the ball to second on two hops.

McCracken walked the first batter of the second inning, but that was it. His curve started snapping over the plate at the last second, pitches that had been breaking into the dirt now crossed the plate as strikes at the knees. We led 6–0 after three innings, but McCracken Construction got a run in the fourth, one in the fifth when I dropped a fly ball with two out, and two in the sixth on a single and a long home run by McCracken himself.

I managed to hit another Texas League single, but grounded into an inning-ending double play in the sixth.

McCracken and his team were finally catching on that Roger was little more than a journeyman pitcher with a lot of guile. He had a screwball that floated up to the plate like a powder puff, only to break in on the batter's hands at the last instant, usually resulting in a polite pop-up to the pitcher or shortstop. His fast ball was nothing, and he usually threw it out of the strike zone. But his change-up was a beauty, like carrying the ball to the plate. Roger's motion never changed an iota; a hitter would be finished with his swing and on his way to the bench shaking his head by the time the ball reached the catcher.

The seventh went scoreless. We got a run in the eighth on a double and a single, but McCracken's team got two in the bottom, again aided by my misjudgment of a fly ball. It was obvious that Roger was tired. His face was streaked with sweat and grime. His bronze hair appeared wet and wild when he took off his cap, which was after almost every pitch now. To compound matters, we went out on four pitches in the ninth, allowing Roger only about two minutes' rest between innings.

The first batter in the last of the ninth hit a clean single up the middle. The next sacrificed him to second. The third batter swung very late on a change-up and hit it like a bullet just to the right of first. Our first baseman, Lindy Dean, lunged for the ball and, completely by accident, it ended up in his glove. He threw to Roger from a sitting position for the second out. The runner advanced to third.

McCracken was at the plate. As he dug in he sent a steady stream of words toward the mound. Though I couldn't hear, I knew he was baiting Roger. If we lost, there would be at least enough profits from the concessions to pay everyone off, and buy Roger a bus ticket for somewhere not too far away. All I hoped was that the ball wouldn't be hit to me. I didn't mind batting in a tight situation, but defense was my weakness.

McCracken, even though he was right-handed, hammered one to right field on a 2–2 count. Right down the foul line. I actually ran in a step or two before I judged it properly. Then I ran frantically down the line, my back to the plate. I almost overran it. The ball nearly hit me on the head as it plunked onto the soft grass a foot outside the foul line.

Surely he won't hit to the opposite field again, I thought.

Roger gave him a fast ball in the strike zone. It was, of course, the last pitch McCracken was expecting. He swung late, but only late enough to send it to right-center field. I gratefully let the center fielder handle it for the final out.

At our bench Roger wiped his face and hair with a towel.

"You get the rest of the gate receipts and the concession money," he said. "One of McCracken's men will count it with you."

"You didn't bet against us, did you?" I stammered.

"Of course not. I bet it all *on* us."

"What if we'd lost?"

"It wouldn't be the first time I've left a town on foot with people throwing things at me."

Roger collected his winnings from the president of the university and stuffed the stacks of bills into his equipment bag. He settled his debts and bought the team supper and unlimited ice cream at the Springtime Café. He tipped Mrs. Richards ten dollars. While Stan and I again turned our backs, he opened the safe and stuffed it full of bills.

"I'll be on the road before daylight," he said. He gave Stan and me an extra twenty each.

Though I was dead tired, I forced myself to only half sleep; I jumped awake every time the old house creaked in the night. I was up and at the window as soon as I heard Roger's steps on the stairs. As I suspected, he did not leave immediately, but again took the tools from the trunk and hoisted them to his shoulder, being careful not to let them rattle. There had been a heavy thundershower about ten o'clock and the air was still pure and sweet as springwater.

I was waiting by the Caddy when Roger returned. His clothes were soiled, his shoes ruined by mud.

"You been in a fight or what?" I said.

"I think you know where I've been," he said, keeping his voice low.

"I know a little about distances," I said.

"When did you suspect?" he asked.

"I measured the distance on your practice field out at Barons'," I said. "Sixty-one feet from the rubber to the plate. No wonder your arm's big as a telephone pole."

"You figure on telling McCracken?"

"No."

"I mean, if you feel you have to it's okay. Just wait until morning."

"I'm not going to," I said.

Roger deposited the tools in the trunk. He began to fiddle with the combination of the safe.

"You don't have to give me anything."

"I want to. I've been working this scam for ten years. No one ever cottoned onto it before. I must be getting careless."

He took about an inch of bills off the top of the pile and handed them to me.

"You really don't need to. Money can't buy what I want."

"Which is?"

"I want this girl I know to like me just the way I am."

"No, money can't do that. But it'll buy a hell of a lot of ice cream." His face broke open into that grin of his that could charm a bone out of a hungry dog's mouth.

"It's all a matter of distances," Roger said from inside the Caddy. "Des Moines to Memphis is 623 miles, less about 110 to Onamata is 513. I'll have a late breakfast in Memphis."

Roger smiled again, reached his right hand up and out the window to shake my hand.

"Maybe we'll run into each other again, Gid. Be cool. It's all a matter of distances. Make them work for you." The window purred up and the car eased away. The only sound it made was gravel crunching under the wide tires.

Reports Concerning the Death of the Seattle Albatross Are Somewhat Exaggerated

THE FIVE P.M. NEWS is doing a feature story on me. Jean Enerson, the beautiful Channel Five anchorwoman, is reading from her TelePrompTer.

"Mike Street, the man inside the Seattle Albatross costume for the past five years, has announced his retirement," she is saying.

"Albatross flies the coop" was how the headline of the *Post-Intelligencer* sports section read.

The camera cuts to the smiling but vacuous face of Buzz Hinkman, the Seattle Mariners' coordinator of public relations.

"The only reason we're making a statement at all is because of the bizarre rumors that have been circulating," says Buzz. "Mike joked that it was time for him to seek visible employment. He's left Seattle and is taking a long holiday while he mulls over a number of employment offers."

In that way of news broadcasters, Buzz goes on talking, mouthing his pompous platitudes while the voice of Jean Enerson lists a few highlights of my career and wishes me well. The final word, however, belongs to Buzz: "I want to assure the press, our own Seattle Mariners fans, and the baseball world at large that reports concerning the death of the Seattle Albatross are somewhat exaggerated." Here Buzz smiles his empty but winning smile for at least the tenth time, and Channel Five moves on to a story about a baby orangutan.

Buzz probably believes what he has just said. And if he doesn't believe it he's not a bad actor. I'm sure the word has been passed down to him from the general manager, perhaps even the owners, who in turn have been briefed by higher powers as to what to say.

The first thing I have to admit is that our people did not understand the civilization of Earth very well. I'm afraid the bureaucrats on our planet aren't very bright, which shouldn't come as any surprise, except that everyone here on Earth accepts as fact that other civilizations are far more intelligent. About the only advantage I have over people on Earth is a built-in ability to engage, with considerable help, in teleportative space travel. If our politicians and military bureaucrats had been smarter, they would have investigated conditions much more thoroughly before packing me off to Earth.

One of the first things we saw when we began intercepting television signals from Earth was the San Diego Chicken.

"Look! Look!" our prime minister chortled. "They have an integrated society. It appears that fifty thousand people on Earth are gathered together to worship one of our own." I have to admit that that *is* what it looked like.

As the TV signals became clearer, the prime minister and the joint chiefs of staff spent a great deal of time watching baseball, not that they understood the game. I've been here for five years and I barely understand it. But what they did understand was popularity, and mascots were popular. The San Diego Chicken was most like one of our own, but B. J. Bird from Toronto, Fred Bird the Red Bird from St. Louis, and even the Phillie Phanatic could walk down the street in any of our major cities without being stared at.

"They even have economically disadvantaged segments of the population," enthused the prime minister, after viewing the bedraggled set of mascots fielded by the Chicago White Sox.

I have to admit I was a natural for the job. I am a bit of an exhibitionist; I had also studied theater, where I majored in pantomime and clowning. Unfortunately, for once the bureaucrats decided to move with extreme haste. Almost before I knew it, I was teletransported to New York City, where, I was informed, there was a school for mascots.

Most of the officials on our planet understood that on Earth mascots weren't real, but just as some children believe cartoon characters really exist, a number of politicians and most of the military believed the mascots were really long lost descendants of ours.

"The thing you're going to have to get used to," one of the bureaucrats said to me, "is that you *never* take off your costume."

"I don't have a costume," I said.

I was given some curious looks by the joint chiefs of staff, the head of External Security, and perhaps even the prime minister.

"Need I remind you that on Earth only people in elaborate costumes look like me?"

"Of course," they said.

My natural colors are blue and white, so it was decided that after I oriented myself to New York and attended mascot school, I'd align myself with the Seattle Mariners, a baseball team that didn't have a mascot.

New York was a great place to start my life on Earth. In the theater district, where the mascot school was located, no one gave me a second glance as I walked the streets. I was given a more than adequate supply of currency, including one delightful hundred-dollar bill that reproduced itself on command. I was able to live in a comfortable hotel and eat at quality restaurants, although my greatest joy was to go to a fish market, buy a tub of sardines, toss them in the air one at a time, and catch them in my mouth.

At the ballpark, after I officially became the Seattle Albatross, I used to use fish in my act. I'd go down to the Pike Street Market and buy a couple of pounds of smelts, then run around the stands tossing fish in the air and swallowing them. Kids would stop me and ask, "You don't really swallow those raw fish, do you?" or, "Are those real fish, or are they made of something else?"

"They're real," I'd say. "Want me to breathe on you?" The kids would shriek and pretend to be afraid of me as I puffed up my cheeks. Then I'd reach way down into my mouth and pull out a smelt. "Have a fish," I'd yell, and chase the kids along the aisles, holding a fish by the tail.

The only recognizable foreign object I brought to Earth with me was my communicating device, a sophisticated sending-receiving set, which, once I was settled in Seattle, lived under my kitchen sink, mixed in with a bag of potatoes, looking exactly like a potato except that it felt like chamois to the touch.

There must have been sixty people at mascot school.

"I never take off my clothes in public," I wrote on my application, for I had decided to remain mute until I became acclimatized. "It's my way of getting into character." The school officials were more interested in the hundred-dollar bills I produced to pay the tuition than in my idiosyncracies. The other students thought I was showing off at first. But I was good at what I did and they soon accepted me. The result was that while a roomful of people in jeans, track suits, and leotards practiced pratfalls and somersaults, I performed in full costume.

What did I look like? Picture the soulful expression of the San Diego Chicken, but picture real feathers, sleek, a brilliant white, like sun on hoarfrost, violet tail feathers and bars of violet along my folded blue wings, and sturdy legs the color of ripe corn. I always wore furry shoes, big as pillows, covered in blue velvet, to keep my bird's feet hidden from the curious.

The thing the Mariners were most interested in was that I would work for free. All they asked me to do was sign a waiver to the effect that if I was injured while performing they would not be liable.

"To what do you attribute your huge success?" the press repeatedly asked me. "You have replaced the San Diego Chicken as the most in-demand performer of your kind in America. What is the secret of the Seattle Albatross?"

"The mystique of the Seattle Albatross is the very elusiveness of my character. None but a select and specific few have ever seen the Mike Street who resides inside this costume. That makes me a mysterious entity and automatically doubles or triples the interest in me."

"Don't you ever secretly yearn for the fame and publicity Ted Giannoulas receives as the San Diego Chicken?" asked Steve Kelly of the *Seattle Times*. "He's a celebrity even when he appears out of costume."

"Oh," and here I would giggle my famous high-pitched laugh-shriek for which I was famous, "just yesterday I spent a lovely day at the Pike Street Market, and just walked around downtown Seattle, relaxing, being myself, *not* having to be a celebrity every minute. I enjoy the private side of my life very much. I wouldn't trade it for anything."

"What about your personal life?"

"I keep my personal and professional life completely separate. My friends guard my privacy with great loyalty and determination."

What the reporter was trying to establish, in a none too subtle way, was my sexual situation. The rumors about me were legion. The most prevalent, of course, was that I was gay. I do have a high speaking voice and a girlish giggle. Apparently at least two young men in Seattle's gay community claimed to be me, and since there were never any denials — "The private life of the Seattle Albatross is private" was my final word on the matter — they are to my knowledge still claiming it. What they will do now that I've officially left Seattle is not my problem. My problem right now is much more serious than that.

My problem then was acute loneliness. And frustration, both sexual and otherwise. No one on my home planet knew exactly the kind of information they wanted me to channel back to them. One high official had the nerve to ask me to bring back Ronald McDonald's autograph. Opportunities for sexual contact were everywhere, but I was unable to make even a close friendship for fear of giving away my secret. I kept an apartment on Union Street which I visited once a week to pick up mail. I occasionally invited a friend or reporter there. I kept canned food in the cupboards, kept the closets full of human clothes, left Willie Nelson albums lying about on the carpet. When I was alone I was able to contrast my position to that of a famous television character. There was an alien named Mork who made wonderful, insane jokes and had a very beautiful woman in love with him. The woman knew what he was but loved him anyway. Mork was always in a lot of trouble, but he was *never* lonely. Except when I was performing, I was utterly lonely.

And even performing had its risks. The closest call I ever had was on an evening when Phil Bradley, Seattle's best outfielder, hit a mammoth home run in the bottom of the ninth inning to bring Seattle a come-from-behind victory. The fans were jubilant, raucous, their adrenaline running high. A whole contingent of them were waiting for me as I made my way down a ramp toward the dressing rooms. It had been a difficult evening for me. While children always loved me, were able to accept the fantasy of me, teenagers were wary and distrustful, somehow aware that I was too real. One had snatched a feather from my wing about the sixth inning. Others had, in more than a joking tone, spoken of tearing off my costume and revealing the real Mike Street.

"Let's get him," several of them screamed.

"Hit him high and hit him low," someone else said.

I tried to run, but I'm not very speedy. Those pursuing me were the same ones who had taunted me earlier, sensing my strangeness. They backed me into a corner. I considered flying. I could soar to the roof in an instant. Better to reveal my identity than die.

"Help!" I yelped, my voice high and shrill. I flapped my wings and tried to fly over their heads. My wings made monstrous beating sounds. Some of them retreated. I scraped my back on the sprinklers in the ceiling of the passageway.

One of them grabbed my legs. I shrieked like a macaw. I struck one hard with my left wing, knocking him down. But they over-powered me.

"Twist his head off," yelled one.

"Wring his neck," cried another. And they fully intended to.

I was scuffling my feet together, trying to expose one scaly foot with its long, razorlike spur. I was going to do several of those barbarians serious damage.

But at that instant two Kingdome security men appeared and rescued me.

From that day on, whenever there were fans in the Dome, there was a security person somewhere close to me.

In 1981 there was a mascots convention in Cleveland in conjunction with the All-Star Game. The San Diego Chicken and I stood out as the class of the field. The minor-league mascots were there too: a real live dog from Cedar Rapids, Iowa, whose stock in trade was to stand frozen, leg in the air, forever in anticipation, in front of a plastic fireplug. What that act had to do with being the mascot of a baseball team still puzzles me.

There was a character there called the Eel, a very thin man who wore a plastic and rubber suit and a bulletlike helmet with red, blinking eyes. He had batteries of some kind hidden inside his flippers and would pass charges of blue electricity from hand to hand as he stood along the baselines. He was, he explained to me, an electric eel.

The men and boys inside those costumes were a strange lot, furtive and uncomfortable when their disguises were peeled away. Several congratulated me for my fortitude in never taking off my costume. Each intimated that he wished he could do the same. Outside their costumes the other mascots were as pale and sad-eyed as velvet portraits, whispering, gentle men happy only when hidden.

But the women. They were everywhere, bright as freshly cut flowers. They couldn't keep their hands off us. Room keys and slips of paper emblazoned with lipsticked phone numbers were thrust into our hands, wings, flippers, beaks, mouths. It must be a significant comment on American masculinity that thousands of women are ready, willing, and able, and aggressively pursue the opportunity to go to bed with men whose physical features are perpetually hidden from sight by the costume of a chicken, bear, eel, cardinal, or some other grotesque caricature of a stuffed toy.

I wonder what these girls and women thought when they stripped away the costume of the Birmingham Bear and found a man of fifty-five, an ex-jockey, his face the color of concrete, his mirthless mouth like a crack in a sidewalk.

But we were not all trailed by women. There was a boy in a fish costume, his tail flapping in the dust, who must have given off an odor to betray that when, as part of his act, he kissed umpires and third-base coaches, it was because he liked umpires and third-base coaches.

In spite of the numerous temptations to sexual pleasure, I never wavered. Sometimes when I was very lonely I would take one or two of my admirers to dinner, but I always went home alone, turning aside, with as much kindness as I could muster, the invitations. For almost five years I behaved impeccably, denied my sexuality. Until I met Virginia.

Most of the players tolerated me. Some even considered me a good luck charm, good-naturedly rubbing my head for luck before going to the plate. Coaches and managers who had not known mascots in their playing days were less accommodating.

"Stay away from the third-base coach," the players warned me, my first year with the team. "He has no sense of humor."

One part of my act was to stand behind the third-base coach's box and parody the signs he was giving. Eventually he was supposed to turn and hit me with a roundhouse right, whereupon I would fall as if unconscious, legs and wings spread wide.

"Maggie," as the players called the third-base coach, was surly and uncooperative from the start.

"Listen, shithead," he said to me, "I only do this because management says I have to," and he smiled a wicked little smile, showing his snuff-stained teeth. I expected an elaboration, but none was forthcoming, until one evening during a pitching change he stalked to the dugout, returned with a bat, and went for my head as if it were a ball on a batting tee.

I think he believed I was somewhere deep within the costume, that my feathered head was empty, my blinking pink eyes controlled by a battery. Otherwise I doubt that he would have tried to kill me in front of twenty thousand fans.

The bat flattened my ruby-red comb. I was in terrible pain, but tried not to let on. I danced like a maniac. The fans loved it. I flew to the top of the dugout and leapt into the arms of the best-looking woman in that section of the stands.

"Kiss it better," I wailed.

The woman obliged. I massaged her breasts with my free wing. She didn't object, in fact she clutched me to her. I love the smell of perfume. It has not yet been invented on my planet.

The fans roared their approval. But if the bat had struck a half inch lower it could easily have disabled me. What would have happened if a doctor had attempted to remove my head in order to examine me?

How I got the name Mike Street. When I walked into the Mariners corporate offices at 100 South King Street and went to introduce myself, my mind went blank. Martin Gardiner was the name the bureaucrats had chosen for me. It was the name I had used in New York, but in New York I had pretended to be mute. For the first time, my speech would be monitored. Suffice it to say that speech on my home planet is fraught with zs and vs and a sound, *uuvvzz*, that is not quite comparable to anything in English.

"Good morning," I said. "My name is . . ." and I panicked. All I could recall was an advertisement I'd seen for the Pike Street Market. ". . . Pike Street, I'd like to —" but the secretary cut me off.

"About ten or twelve blocks straight north on First Avenue," she said, assuming I was asking directions.

"No, no," I said, "my name."

"Your name is Pike Street?"

"Yes. No. Mike Street," I said in desperation. And so it was.

I didn't get to see management that day. In fact, they were downright rude to me.

"The contest isn't until Sunday," the secretary said, eyeing me up and down, her eyes getting large as I riffed the indigo feathers around my neck.

"Contest?" I said.

"The Mascot Contest," she said, her voice incredulous. "Sunday afternoon at the Kingdome. Here are the rules." She handed me a mimeographed page containing several paragraphs of dark print below the Mariners logo.

A contest. I was going to have to compete for a job.

"You shouldn't wear your costume now," the secretary was saying. "You'll get it dirty before Sunday."

I wandered out onto the street, where, instead of trying to be inconspicuous, which was impossible, I flaunted myself, nuzzling children and attractive women, taking pratfalls, pretending to swallow a parking meter.

On Sunday there was a large crowd at the Kingdome. A mascot's costume was good for free admission. There were about forty of us, from children dressed in Halloween costumes to two or three dressed in elaborate and expensive get-ups that rivaled my own real self. There were also three or four very odd individuals who, I suspect, were inmates, escaped or otherwise, from some institution.

We were herded in a flock, or whatever a collective of mascots would be called. Perhaps a *plush* of mascots would be appropriate, for many were direct imitations of the San Diego Chicken, the Phillie Phanatic, or B. J. Bird.

The contest was a fiasco. The majority of participants had no stage presence whatsoever, and, after we were admitted to the playing field, merely plodded across the outfield toward second base.

Besides myself there was a man on stilts dressed as the Space Needle, a magnificent and imaginative creation, but he was not cuddly or lovable, and was ill equipped to run or take face-first dives into the infield dirt.

Perhaps the most unusual was an entry I called Mr. Baby, a middle-aged, bald, pudgy man, who was dressed in a massive diaper with the Mariners logo stenciled on the back, and a frilly bonnet. We talked briefly while we waited to be admitted to the playing field.

"A dream come true. A dream come true," he kept repeating. "It has always been my fantasy to appear as a baby in front of the whole world. I dress like this in private all the time. My wife is really very understanding. Sometimes she dusts me with talcum powder while

I lay back on my blanket and kick and gurgle. Tell me, do you wear your costume in the privacy of your own home? Does it have sexual meaning for you?"

"I do wear it at home," I said, "and I suppose it has as much sexual meaning as any other costume."

"I think perhaps we understand each other," Mr. Baby said, with what I interpreted as an ominous tone.

When the limping, slovenly parade of mascots began, Mr. Baby dropped to his hands and knees and crawled slowly, like a grotesque toy, toward the infield. Unfortunately, the sharp bristles of the artificial turf soon proved too much for Mr. Baby's tender hands and knees, and he began to bleed. Our bedraggled troupe of would-be clowns was not monitored in any way. While I and several others in our group, including a girl dressed as Raggedy Ann, waited for someone to intercept Mr. Baby and say, "That's enough," he continued to crawl like a huge slug across the toothbrush-like carpet until he began leaving a trail of blood behind him on the pale green surface.

"I think you should stop now," I said to him, but he stared up at me, his big baby eyes overflowing with tears, but filled also with pain and ecstasy.

"A dream come true," he repeated over and over as he crawled beside me, a fine spray of blood spattering on my plush feet.

A man wearing a moth-eaten satyr's head and a canvas raincoat stopped along the third-base line, and, flinging open the coat, exposed himself to six or seven thousand fans. The fans booed his efforts until eventually a couple of security guards appeared and escorted him off the field.

The judges were Miss Elliott Bay, a toothy girl in a blue and white bathing suit and a Mariners cap, and a disc jockey named Dr. Slug, whose stock in trade was slime jokes: "What is a slug's favorite song?" Slime on My Hands. "What is a slug's favorite novel?" *Slime and Punishment.* "Who is a slug's favorite playwright?" Neil Slimon. "What creeps slowly toward the new year?" Father Slime.

The judges chose seven of us and lined us up at second base, where the baseball fans were to choose a winner by means of applause. There were prizes to be won, with the final winner getting to be Seattle Mascot for one game.

The applause set three of us apart: me, the Space Needle, and something called the Kitsap Carp, a person of indeterminate sex dressed in a fish costume. A large and vocal group of fans kept chanting, "We want the flasher," and I can't help but feel that he was the people's choice, for after all, what is it we value most but when people expose themselves unashamedly to us, though we also fear them for it?

I could tell that in spite of my alabaster feathers, my endearing pink eyes as big as sunflowers, and the indigo and violet shading along my neck and wings, that I was not going to win the contest unless I did something spectacular. In the first round the Space Needle had received more applause.

"Well, ladies and gentlemen, we've narrowed it down to three finalists," intoned Dr. Slug, who was short, with slick hair, piano legs, and an obscenely protruding belly.

He then proceeded to introduce each of us briefly. The Kitsap Carp turned out to be a woman with a thick accent who said her ambition in life was to make people happy and bring peace to the world. The Space Needle, a professor of economics at Western Washington State University, was active in Big Brothers and a currently fashionable branch of evangelical Christianity. The only all-American thing he hadn't done was give birth.

When my turn came, I pantomimed an inability to speak. I spread my wings to their full span, ruffled my neck feathers, and did a jigging, spinning dance from second base to the pitcher's mound. Flapping my wings, but being careful not to give the impression of actual flight, I ran toward the backstop and leapt — actually I flew about eight feet in the air — and clutched onto the wire mesh. I scaled the screen gracefully, all the time making birdlike whirring sounds. The fans at first cheered my exploits, then became silent as they do in the presence of a daring circus act. I climbed the screen until I could reach a guy wire and proceeded up it claw over claw — or at least I hoped I gave that impression, for I was actually flying. I climbed up to the concrete roof of the Kingdome. Giving my loud natural call, *"Uuvvzzz,"* I leapt from the guy wire to another that controlled the raising and lowering of the baseball scoreboard. The crowd gasped. From there I jumped and, with one flap of my delicate wings, was able to grasp onto a piece of the red, white, and blue bunting that hung down from the compression ring at the top of the Dome.

I then made a complete circle, swinging from one piece of bunting to the next. I must have looked like a feathered monkey. I crowed loudly as the fans cheered and applauded. The circle finished, I leapt back to the guy wire and descended, claw over claw again.

When the applause was monitored I was virtually a unanimous winner.

"Ladies and gentlemen, I give you Mike Street, the Seattle Albatross," cried Dr. Slug.

It was a woman who was my downfall, or perhaps I should say it was her downfall that led to my downfall. Her name was Virginia and she was much more persistent than most of the young women who flaunted themselves and fluttered after me like butterflies.

She was waiting for me after a game, in the passageway behind the Mariners dugout. How she got there was anybody's guess. She wanted to take me to dinner. She flattered me. Residents of my planet are all susceptible to flattery. I finally agreed. Without asking, she chose a fish restaurant, pointing it out as one of the many things we had in common. And we did have common interests. What she had that interested me was intelligence, something one seldom encounters in players, fans, or mascot groupies.

"Why do you like me?" I asked.

"You're mysterious," she said.

"So are a lot of people who don't hide in albatross costumes. What if I took this off and you found me horribly disfigured? What if I was really an alien with skin the color of chianti, several eyes, and a tail?"

"You have a cute lisp, Mike," she said. "Your trouble is you're just shy. I can tell. I can also tell when someone is very lonely."

She was certainly right about that. I was desperately lonely. And she was extremely pretty. She was twenty-two years old, with blue eyes and a beautiful tan, and she also wore an exotic perfume that made my heart beat like a motorcycle engine. Her dress smelled freshly ironed, and she wore tiny white shoes with her red toenails peeping out.

It had been three months since I had heard from my home planet. After my first dinner with Virginia, I went against rules and contacted them. Someone unknown to me answered. The line was full of static, like a million throat clearings.

"We've updated our equipment," the voice told me. "Your communicator is obsolete."

"Then bring me home."

"There seems to be a problem," the voice went on. "Someone is working on it. We'll be in touch in due course."

I demanded to speak with my previous contact.

"He is no longer with us."

I asked for any of the joint chiefs of staff, for the prime minister.

"All gone," I was informed. "Retired or replaced. Space exploration is not a priority with this administration."

"Then send me a female for company," I pleaded. "I could live here if I had a partner. We could work as a team —"

"Impossible," replied the voice. "We suggest you attune yourself to interstellar living for the foreseeable future. And, incidentally, don't call us, we'll call you."

I had no sooner hidden the communicator among the sprouting potatoes when Virginia came tapping at my door. I was charmed by her. She talked in bright bursts of sound like splashes of bird song. I didn't let her inside, but I took her out for ice cream. All the time we were together I was rationalizing that since she was sweet and intelligent I might be able to forget for once that I was an alien. I mean, our method of sexual gratification is not *that* different from what is engaged in here on Earth.

We had dinner for three consecutive nights. Virginia was a public relations trainee for Boeing. She wrote optimistic press releases in what she called "media-oriented language."

Each night, at the end of our date, I clowned a bit in the lobby of her apartment building, bowed, hugged her in a friendly, brotherly way, pecked her cheek, and bolted out the door before I lost control of myself.

"Can we go back to your place?" Virginia asked after our fourth date. We had been interrupted about ten times during our meal as I signed menus, napkins, scraps of paper, and children. Adults produced cameras from unlikely places on their bodies and then thrust reluctant older children into my arms for picture-taking purposes.

I should have turned Virginia's request aside with a joke, but I didn't. I was thinking with my reproductive system.

"Rather than my apartment, why don't I show you my special place? I'd like you to see the very top of the Kingdome at night."

Though I kept the apartment for show, I actually had lived for four years in the compression ring at the top of the Kingdome. It was a perfect aerie for a large, solitary bird.

Inside the Kingdome, two dim night lights burned.

"Once your eyes become accustomed, it's like deep twilight," I said to Virginia.

"You mean we're going up there," she said, after I pointed to the compression circle at the top.

"It's two hundred and fifty feet," I said. "But my nest is there. I've never told another soul about this, Virginia."

She laughed prettily.

"You're crazy," she said. "I can't wait to see what you really look like."

"Then let's not wait," I said.

"How do we get up there? Is there an elevator?"

"There is a traditional mechanical way to get there. But let's not be traditional." I scooped her up in my wings. "Hang on tightly to my neck," I said. I ran a few steps to gain momentum, then my long blue wings flapped like blankets snapping in a strong wind, and we soared toward the roof of the Kingdome. I landed with great agility, not even ruffling Virginia's hair.

"How did you do that?" Virginia squealed.

"It's all done with mirrors," I said.

"Wow!" She looked about at my few possessions, the pole I used as my roost. Unfortunately, there was rather a mess below the pole. I hadn't been expecting company.

"God, it looks like a giant bird lives here," said Virginia, and then the significance of what she had said struck her. She stared at me with a new curiosity, a curiosity mixed with fear.

"I was hoping you'd roost with me," I said, knowing as the words escaped how strange and futile I must have sounded. Virginia stared searchingly at me a moment longer; her expression changed; she stepped back two steps and screamed. Her voice reverberated eerily through the empty dome, which frightened her even more.

I could see that she would be in serious danger if she stepped any farther back. I lunged at her. She, of course, misinterpreted my movement as one of hostility. An instant later, she was hurtling toward the baseball field, her death scream a small, sad sound in the heavy air.

I launched myself after her, but there was no way I could catch up with her falling form. When I reached the artificial turf, she lay dead near second base, blood seeping outward from her grotesquely sprawled corpse.

I knew at once that I couldn't risk involvement. Panic-stricken, I ran, not even thinking that my secret living quarters would surely be discovered, that Virginia's small, red-and-white striped handbag was lying on the floor of the aerie.

At first, the police were very nice, cordial even. I was contacted routinely about Virginia's death. But I am a very bad criminal, or at least I am very bad at concealing information. I didn't have a *story*.

"Do you know Virginia Knowlton?" they asked.

"We were good friends," I said.

The police had the Kingdome maintenance people take them to the top of the dome. There they found my roost, the evidence that I used the space as living quarters. But for some reason the connection was not made. Police deal with cold facts; the fantastical seldom crosses their mind.

Virginia's death was given sensational treatment by the press. I was dogged by reporters, radio and television crews. It is very difficult for someone as colorfully unique as I to hide, anywhere.

I maintained silence. I shrugged my shoulders at all questions. I pecked at microphones and licked the lenses of probing TV cameras.

At my apartment, I went against orders and contacted my home planet. If anything, the static was more tenacious than ever. I explained my predicament.

"Carry on as usual," came the reply.

"Bring me home," I wailed.

"We find your situation interesting," the garbled voice replied. "We will study your request and get back to you in good time. Please don't try to contact us again. We are changing frequencies to something beyond the capabilities of your communicator."

I was interviewed a number of times at police headquarters. They were very nice. I think they believed me. I admitted to taking Virginia up to see the top of the Kingdome. She was overcome by the height, fell before I could save her. I panicked and ran.

Since there were no other marks or wounds on her body, and since we were known to be good friends, the police finally announced they were closing the case, marking it as 'death by misadventure.'

"There is one thing," a detective named Art said to me. "You'll have to let us have a look at the real you. You know, just in case you fought or something. Wouldn't want to find you with scratches all over your body."

"But this is the real me," I said plaintively.

"It's only a formality," said the detective. "Please don't give us any trouble at this late date, Mr. Street."

"I can't."

"You mean won't."

"I never let anyone see me. I carry pictures . . ." I fumbled for the ID I kept taped out of sight.

"Sorry," said Art, and he and his partner moved toward me. His partner grabbed me firmly by the shoulders.

"Just take off the top of the costume and let us see your head. We promise not to tell anyone what you look like," said the big detective.

He grabbed my neck and began looking for snaps or buttons.

"Does this thing screw on and off?"

I could tell by the tone of his voice as he said it that he was beginning to be suspicious.

"No! No!" I shrieked, and slipped from his grasp, his hands sliding down my feathers as though I were greased. The door to the room was closed, and Art stood arms folded across his chest, blocking any escape.

The window. I reverted entirely to my natural state. I flew against the window, hard. I chittered and squawked. I kicked off one of my plush boots; the talons on my feet, which had never been unfurled in my five years on Earth, slashed the air, striking anything within their reach.

A detective clutched at one of my legs. I struck, ripping away a lapel from his jacket and gashing his chest with the same movement. Blood appeared, bright as neon. But I could not escape. The big detective broke one of my long wings with a karate blow. I crashed, hissing and screaming, to the floor.

Both men had guns trained on me. I remained still.

"I think we'd better call the chief in on this," the big one said.

The chief called the FBI. The FBI called the Pentagon.

I am being held in an isolation cell, somewhere inside Fort Lewis military base outside of Tacoma.

Buzz Hinkman is now fielding questions from a collective of reporters. It is interesting to me that the disappearance of a baseball team's mascot should be news. Buzz is smiling and repeating the phrase about my opting for a visible occupation. Buzz is not smart enough to have thought of that himself, and the FBI and military types I have been subjected to the past few days are totally humorless. Perhaps the FBI employs a joke writer.

My wing is healing nicely. I have refused to talk with any of the men in tight suits from the FBI, or the finger-pointing military men with crew cuts, who fire questions at me in a staccato whir.

"We have recovered everything from your apartment," a steely eyed officer told me this morning. "So as not to create a suspicious situation, we hired Allied Van Lines to go in and pack everything. Even had them move it all to an address in San Francisco before we seized it."

He stared at me in silence for a long time, as though expecting a compliment from me for his intelligent behavior.

They obviously have my communicating device, though they haven't mentioned it to me. I'm sure it is sitting on a velvet pillow in some airtight, germ-free, anti-explosive box.

I like to imagine that every other baseball mascot in the nation has been whisked out of his apartment in the dead of night and is, somewhere in the bowels of the Pentagon, being dusted, tested, poked, and prodded. Perhaps right now whole truckfuls of Ronald McDonalds, Mr. Peanuts, and all the characters from Sesame Street are being interrogated by a paranoid military. In fact, a few hours ago, one of my interrogators made the word association — Mike Street — Sesame Street — smiled cunningly, and slipped out of this heavily locked room.

The interview with Buzz Hinkman is over. The Channel Five news team are all on camera. Tony Ventrella, the sportscaster, is about to deliver his segment of the news, but before he does he produces from under the anchor desk a reasonable likeness of my head, done in plush and papier-mâché.

"Jean and Jeff," he says, "I've been keeping something from you all these years. I'm really the Seattle Albatross." The three of them smile their charming smiles.

"That's quite a confession, Tony," says Jean. "I suppose it's rather like getting an albatross off your neck."

The three of them laugh charming laughter.

"Back in a moment with all the sports," says Tony. Then, as his face fades into a lawn-and-garden fertilizer commercial, he adds, "Good luck, Mike Street, wherever you are."

The
Further Adventures
of Slugger McBatt

For Retlaw Erohs

EVERYONE who is ridiculed, for whatever reason, develops a way of handling that ridicule. A refuge. I found mine in cartoon art.

At eleven I would have given anything to have been athletically inclined. It is a terrible shame that boys place so much emphasis on athletic prowess at that age. At twenty-five it doesn't matter in the least if a person is sink-chested, physically weak, unable to swim, skate, ride a bicycle, do gymnastic exercises, catch, or bat a baseball. But when I was growing up, it was not only very important; it was all-important.

My ineptness at sports was partially physical and partially mental. As a young child I suffered several serious illnesses that left me underweight and weak. I had fine bones and was delicately constructed. I also had parents who, although poor, were interested in the arts and didn't encourage me toward athletics. Physical exertion and roughhousing never appealed to me.

As early as fourth grade I realized that participation in athletics was of no concern to most adults, and since my interest in books led me into an adult world, I made no attempt to compete with my peers, or even to participate at all.

I also found that being completely inept at something is a kind of success. If you are going to be bad at something, then be the worst. Laugh at your own failure. Still, being an outsider was no fun.

In sixth grade we studied art for the first time, and I quickly realized I had a sense of depth perception and color most everyone lacked. The teacher praised my work in front of the whole class. But art was considered a *girl's* subject, so my skill didn't impress the boys.

My grudging acceptance came about in a strange way. I guess I really did crave it, for though I was the most inept athlete in the school I tagged along when our baseball team played a game across town one day. We were beaten very badly, something like 31–4, and I can't say I felt bad. It was not unpleasant to see the same boys who taunted me about my lack of athletic ability look like fools on the field, or to see our star pitcher, Freddie MacLeish, a chief tormentor of mine, have his every pitch driven for extra base hits.

I still don't quite understand why I did what I did next: after the game, as we were heading for the bus line, I took a piece of brick and printed on the sidewalk, GROVER CLEVELAND STINKS!, in six-inch-high, orange letters. I had nothing against Grover Cleveland; in fact I was rather pleased that they had beaten my school so badly. A confrontation soon ensued, with several boys from Grover Cleveland anxious to pulverize me, and my own team only marginally in favor of protecting me.

It was at this point, strictly out of a spirit of self-preservation, that, with the brick fragment still in my hands, I knelt on the sidewalk again and drew an outline of the half-dozen angry Grover Cleveland ballplayers who were clustered around me.

They were able to recognize themselves and were not displeased.

"Hey, Buford, that's you," one of them said to a bulldog-faced boy who hovered over me.

"That's you, Sarkesian," said somebody else. "Geez, see how he got your beak."

"Draw me, kid," commanded the left fielder, a short, slow-footed boy with a Babe Ruth belly.

I sketched him in, giving him more muscles and less fat.

"Pretty good, kid."

They kept me drawing for half an hour. I even sketched some of my own players, and ended with about forty feet of sidewalk covered with orange sketches. I was forgiven completely after I drew a tank, taking up two sidewalk squares, its long gun barrel spitting brick-colored fire.

"You guys should send over an art team," one of the Grover Cleveland players said. "You sure as hell can't play baseball." Our bus arrived and we all parted on good terms.

A few of the boys even talked to me on the bus ride home, though they were puzzled by my self-destructive show of bravado.

It was only a week or two later when I had a chance to show off my artistic skills for a second time.

Opposites attract. We are often drawn toward people who have qualities we don't, qualities we wish we had. It was like that with Freddie MacLeish. He was the best athlete in our class: he pitched; he could hit a baseball farther than even our coach, Mr. Gault; he could throw a strike from center field to the plate; he could steal bases at will.

Freddie was muscular, his biceps hard. My own arms were long and pale, and no matter how hard I flexed I could raise nothing that even resembled a muscle.

"I guess you just haven't worked yourself hard enough," Freddie would say, marveling at my weakness, my inability to run, throw, or hit. Freddie had spent his first ten years on a dirt farm in southern Missouri and had pitched hay, cut wood, and cleaned barns right alongside his father.

The irony was that I, too, had been raised on a farm. But I had always been sickly and had never engaged in any farm chores more strenuous than feeding the chickens. I was delighted when my family moved to St. Louis, while Freddie missed the country and spent summer vacation on his grandparents' farm.

"Girl's work!" Freddie said contemptuously when I mentioned it.

"My kid sister, Marjorie, fed all the chickens when she was only six years old. And she gathered the eggs, too. You were probably afraid to gather eggs." He eyed me with a mocking stare.

"Of course not," I said, trying to sneer myself. He had no way of checking. Actually, I hated the fierce, orange-eyed hens that pecked at my wrists as I slipped my hands under their slippery feathers. I hated the stifling smells of the hen house and did the job only on threat of punishment.

What did I have to offer Freddie? I was smarter than he was in school. But he wasn't dumb. During study period I helped him with his schoolwork, but not enough to have him in my debt. And I had to be very careful not to make a point of hanging around him, even though we lived in the same block of big old houses near Lafayette Square, for I had seen him turn viciously on other boys whom he deemed *sucks* and embarrass them cruelly in front of whoever was present.

The answer to the question about what I could offer Freddie came one May morning when we were supposed to play baseball in our phys. ed. class. It rained torrentially and we had to stay in the classroom. Mr. Gault had not expected rain, so he had nothing for us to do. He diagrammed a suicide squeeze on the blackboard, then rambled on aimlessly, reading from the *Baseball Rule Book*.

"What do you think will happen in *Ozark Ike?*" an enterprising student asked. *Ozark Ike* was a comic strip in our daily newspaper, about a L'il Abner–type baseball player and his beautiful girlfriend, Dinah. Ike played for the Bugs and was a larger-than-life hero who belted home runs indiscriminately. *Ozark Ike* was not a very good comic strip — even as an eleven-year-old I could tell that.

When I got the opportunity to speak, after a number of boys had talked enthusiastically, running over each other's words to say how wonderful *Ozark Ike* was, I said I thought it was poorly done. Amidst groans, I said what I thought was wrong with it.

"It has no evil, evil characters. What it needs are villains like there are in *Dick Tracy* — the Mole, Flattop, the Brow — to liven it up."

You would have thought I had suggested assassinating the president.

"I suppose you can do better," a number of belligerent faces shouted, mouths moving like fish, lips pulled back from small teeth.

"I suppose I can," I said.

I tore a page from my loose-leaf notebook and, in front of their eyes, created *The Adventures of Slugger McBatt*. I drew four rows of four panels and, while Mr. Gault and my classmates watched, outlined for the first time the shape of Slugger McBatt crouched over the plate, his bat cocked, a ball zooming toward him.

I wasn't a great artist but I had a gift for perspective, at least enough to get by on. I gave McBatt a halo of curly hair that surrounded his face, two large front teeth, and a dimple on each side of his mouth.

"Geez, he looks like Freddie," said one of the boys.

I didn't let on, but I was thrilled to see my ability as a caricaturist recognized. More boys joined in the chorus of approval. I sneaked a look at Freddie; he was smiling broadly, displaying his dimples to full advantage.

I have always been a storyteller. I quickly created a villain to provide the conflict: a squat, hairy, ape-like creature called the Mitt, whose monkey face was inverted like a baseball glove.

I drew the Mitt glowering and muttering from a seat behind home plate. The Mitt had bet millions of dollars against McBatt's team, the Flies, winning the pennant. To be sure the Flies didn't win, the Mitt was going to have to get Slugger McBatt out of the line-up. His plan was to go to the league president and report that McBatt was taking bribes.

At that point, the class ended, but I had won the attention of even the most skeptical, and everyone wanted assurance from me that I would draw more panels for the next time the class met. It was a twice-a-week class. I readily agreed.

I had a new page ready at our next meeting. It was a magnificent high-skied day. Outside the school fence lilacs drooped with large purple coils, perfuming the air. The panels were passed from hand to hand around the backstop. The boys hooted and hollered at each other and particularly at Freddie. I had worked hard and carefully over the new panels, making Slugger McBatt look even more like

Freddie. I gave Slugger Freddie's bulging muscles, and when Slugger was out of uniform, he wore a plaid shirt just like Freddie's. The boys began to call Freddie 'Slugger.' And, when we chose up sides, instead of being the last one picked, as I used to be, I was always chosen second by Freddie, right after he chose his catcher. Everyone nodded and murmured their approval. I had been accepted at last.

My family had lived in the same block as Freddie for a year, but in the tight cliques of childhood friendships and inflexible groupings, he might as well have lived across the city. I was very surprised a couple of days later, a cloudy, windy Saturday, when he called on me for the first time. Following the custom of our neighborhood, he literally *called* on me, standing in the back yard below where my family occupied the third floor of a crumbling house with unpainted siding, and hollered my name, "Artie! Artie!" until I came out the door high above him. A set of rickety wooden stairs on the outside of the building led to our apartment.

He actually invited me to his house. We sat in a dark dining room and leafed through comics and Big Little Books. His mother fed us raspberry pie and milk, and we played a game of Snakes and Ladders. Freddie was as nice as could be.

"You're better than the guy who draws *Ozark Ike*," he said as he looked at the comics. "I like *Slugger McBatt* a lot better."

He hinted that he'd like a peek at my next set of strips, and I didn't say I wouldn't. I didn't know if I could trust Freddie. Once, the previous fall, as I walked by his house where four or five boys were roughhousing in the front yard, he had spoken to me briefly, then showed off his strength by demonstrating a number of wrestling holds on me, making fun of my physical weakness all the while.

When the weather cleared, we went outside and called on several other boys, some of whom weren't even in our class, but being with Freddie assured me acceptance, no questions asked. We played Run-Sheep-Run and Kick the Can. When it was my turn to be *it*, the other boys didn't sneak away a few blocks and set up another game, as they were known to do when someone they didn't like was *it*. Freddie even let me spot and catch him in one game of Hide and Seek.

I let Freddie preview the *Slugger McBatt* strips. Slugger performed superhuman efforts on the field, hitting home runs over the top of the stadium, leaping ten rows deep in the stands to make a final out.

Off the field, when the Mitt couldn't prove that Slugger was taking bribes, he decided to poison the water cooler in the Flies dugout. But Slugger caught him at the last moment, picked him up, and pounded him good, saying something smart about "a lot of pounding just might make him into a good Mitt."

The final panel showed Slugger's good friend Police Chief Rafferty loading a bleeding and battered Mitt into a paddy wagon, while Slugger, looking more like Freddie than ever, stood in the background piously saying, "And may the game of baseball always be a clean and worthwhile sport."

A few blocks from the school was a cardboard box factory, Southern Box Inc., and I had observed that teachers occasionally begged a flat sheet of white cardboard about the size of a newspaper page for class projects. I did the same, shyly showing my comic strip to a foreman among the clatter of presses. He gave me three sheets. Now I was able to draw *Slugger McBatt* in the same format as the Sunday comics.

The boys loved it. I was not unimpressed with my own ability. But I was more excited about being accepted by my peers. It was more fun to be on the inside than the outside. Even my teachers read my comic strip each week and my stock went up with them, too.

I soon invented a new villain, the Bat, a weasel-like creature in the shape of a baseball bat, with beady eyes and long cat whiskers sprouting from the bat handle. He had a pig snout and tiny, sharp teeth. Imitating *Ozark Ike*, I gave Slugger a beautiful, doe-eyed girlfriend with long raven hair, who I drew to resemble Freddie's sister, Marjorie.

I had never had a girlfriend, but Marjorie appealed to me. She was a year younger than I, shy to a point of being almost furtive. She spent a lot of her time petting and grooming two amber rabbits that lived in a pen next to the garage in their back yard. Marjorie had always been nice to me, even before Freddie decided I could be his friend.

One afternoon, Marjorie and a couple of friends were playing a game in the leaf-enveloped back yard when I came to call on Freddie, who, it turned out, was not home. Marjorie invited me to join their game. I don't remember what kind of game it was, but I was able to hold Marjorie's hand as we went through whatever rituals the game required. I would have been happy to stay the whole afternoon if Freddie hadn't come home and rescued me from "those dumb girls."

Another time Marjorie and I sat on an upturned packing box in the back yard while she petted and combed one of her large, docile rabbits. I had vague fantasies of Marjorie touching me with the same affection she showed for the rabbit. I seriously considered leaning over and kissing her; I'm sure she wouldn't have minded. But I didn't.

The weekend before our final week of school it rained heavily all Saturday morning. When I ventured over to Freddie's about two o'clock, the trees were dripping noisily. The odor of honeysuckle filled the wet, fresh air. Dandelions, usually as big as half-dollars and as bright as egg yolks, were closed up, as brown and shriveled as stained thumbs. Mauve and white Lilac petals were scattered across both our yards. Freddie's yard was canopied with cottonwood trees, the sticky leaves as large as a man's hand.

In the back yard I sang out Freddie's name until he appeared at the back door and invited me inside.

The interior of the house was very dark.

"Mom and Dad have gone shopping," Freddie said. His father was a bricklayer with a full head of bushy red hair. The MacLeishes had a very old car, the color of manure, with wooden-spoke wheels.

We made our way through the living room, where Marjorie was playing with cutouts at a circular oak table cluttered with her mother's dressmaking paraphernalia.

Freddie teased Marjorie a little, but she wouldn't be drawn into a fight, and I wouldn't aid Freddie in teasing her.

"Somebody likes somebody," Freddie chanted, and crossed his index fingers one over the other, rubbing them together like two sticks, a gesture I have never understood, even as an adult.

He was right about my liking Marjorie, and I was embarrassed, though she was able to dismiss Freddie's teasing with a small, scornful smile.

Freddie and I went to the basement and for a while we played with his lead soldiers and a cap gun, but we were both getting too old for those kinds of toys.

The basement was a dark and mildewy place with a crumbling concrete floor. Freddie peed into the drain in the middle of the floor. The whole basement stunk of mold and urine.

Bored, we went back upstairs, passing through the living room again, and went into the sun porch at the front of the house.

"Have you ever done it with a girl?" Freddie asked me.

I simply shook my head. I really didn't have any idea what *doing it* involved.

"I did it once," Freddie said confidentially. "You be sure you never repeat this so my parents find out." Again I shook my head mutely. "It was with a girl who lived on the farm next to us. We were out in the fields haying, and she took me up into the supply wagon. She was fourteen."

Freddie waited for me to make some comment, but I just sat, my eyes wide, not sure whether to believe him or not.

"But I'm never gonna do it again until I get married," Freddie said. "Would you like to do it sometime?"

"I don't know."

"You'd like to do it with Marjorie. You like Marjorie, don't you?"

"Sure, I like her, but —" I began in a small voice.

"You should ask Marjorie," he said.

I remained silent, hoping Freddie would change the subject. Eventually he did.

Rain beat a steady tattoo against the foggy windows of the sun porch. There was an old sofa with round arms, weather-stained, smelling of mildew. There were tall stacks of yellowed newspapers against the walls, leaving very little room for us to do anything. We tried rolling a ball back and forth, tried to create a game by batting at it with a discarded calendar roll. Nothing worked. Freddie bounced about exuding energy, becoming more and more agitated.

The wind blew and cottonwood leaves slapped against the windows of the porch. The room became dusky, though it wasn't yet three o'clock. In the living room Marjorie turned on a lamp, and a spine of light slashed across the floor of the porch.

We sat on the sofa, leafing through a tattered old *National Geographic*, most of its pictures cut out to fulfill some social studies project at school.

Suddenly, Freddie's restless energy got the better of him; he seized me and began to wrestle. It was a completely one-sided contest.

"Al 'Mr. Murder' Mills is about to crunch another opponent into submission with his world-famous sleeper hold," he cried, circling my neck in a vicious headlock.

I occasionally talked my father into taking Freddie and me to the wrestling matches, where we watched villains like Al "Mr. Murder" Mills, the Cardiff Giant, and "Logger" Jack McDonald stomp on various good-guy wrestlers.

I didn't try to defend myself. I was no match for Freddie. Usually when he did something like this I just let myself go limp, and he got tired of tormenting me in a couple of minutes.

This time he would not give up. Freddie held me down, twisted an arm behind my back, forced my face deep into the dusty upholstery. He continued his running commentary on wrestling holds as he moved from arm locks to reverse leg holds to toeholds to half and full nelsons.

"You ought to toughen yourself up," he said at one point, flinging me against the cushions like a rag doll.

He got both my hands pinned behind my back, both my wrists clamped in one of his hands.

"Hey, Marjorie," he called suddenly. "Come here and see what we're doing."

Marjorie didn't answer.

"You like Marjorie, don't ya?" Freddie said loudly, knowing his voice would carry easily to the living room. When I didn't reply he applied pressure to my pinioned arms. "Come on, say it," he hissed into my ear.

"I like Marjorie," I said. He wasn't hurting me enough for me to cry, but the frustration was getting to me.

"You hear that, Jorie? Artie says he likes you. Why don't you come in here, Jorie? We got something to show you. Artie's got something to show you. Haven't you, Artie?"

Suddenly his free hand was underneath me, scrabbling at my belt.

I thrashed in complete panic, but I could do nothing. He undid my belt and zipper, then pulled my pants and shorts down to my knees.

Next he turned me over so I was completely exposed to the doorway if Marjorie should come in.

"Hey, Jorie!" he called, his voice loud with excitement. "Artie's got something to show ya. Guess what it is?"

"Freddie, you better behave yourself, or I'll tell Mom," came Marjorie's voice, just a few feet away on the other side of the wall. I suspected that if I really screamed or broke into loud sobs Freddie would let me go. But noise like that could well bring Marjorie onto the porch to see what was going on.

"It's pink, and it rhymes with *think* and *mink* and *clink*" sang Freddie, the sharp, unpleasant odors of his excitement enveloping me. "Come here, Jorie."

My shirt was now pulled up around my chest. I could see the tan line across my belly and thighs. The pale, bluey whiteness of my midsection struck me as incredibly ugly. The barest fuzz of blond hair was beginning to grow in my pubic area.

I struggled wildly but in silence; tears of rage and humiliation poured down my face. I coughed and felt sick to my stomach.

"Well, if you won't come out here guess we'll have to come in there," he said and pulled me to my feet.

"No-ooooo," I wailed, my voice high and thin with terror. I screamed as loud as I could, over and over.

I vaguely heard Marjorie's voice saying, "Freddie! Stop it!"

Freddie released my arms and was saying, "I was only kidding. Stop yelling now."

I suppose I had screamed for only thirty seconds but it seemed like minutes and the echoes of my own voice reverberated wildly in my head, as I covered myself and pulled my clothes into order. I didn't know if Marjorie had come to the doorway or not.

Freddie was plainly annoyed with me. "Can't you even take a joke," he said as he walked through the living room to the kitchen. I could hear the fridge door open. I lay gasping and sobbing on the old sofa, trying to quiet my heart, which was beating as wildly as one of Marjorie's rabbits' when it was frightened.

Then I heard Marjorie's soft voice from the doorway.

"Are you all right, Artie?"

I leapt to my feet as if I had only been play-acting, ignoring the fact that my face and eyes must have been red, my cheeks stained with tears.

"Sure," I said, "he was only fooling around." I couldn't bring myself to say *we*.

Marjorie looked at me dubiously with her big, chocolate eyes. I couldn't tell from her expression whether she had seen anything. "Are you sure?" she said. She had applied some of her mother's lipstick to her thin lips, turning them the sharp pink of a Christmas cactus bloom.

I nodded, signifying that I was okay.

"Did Freddie take your pants down?" she asked. " 'Cause if he did I'll tell Mom and she'll really give it to him."

"No, no," I said too quickly. "He was just joking around. He had my arms pinned down too hard was why I was yelling. But I'm okay now."

Marjorie continued to look dubious. "If you want to talk to Mom when she gets home, come over, or call her on the phone."

We stood looking at each other. I'm sure I was wringing my hands or twisting my shirt into knots. I knew I was never going to come to their house again, ever. I could never face either of them. I couldn't even bear the thought of trekking through the house, of having to pass Freddie. The door from the sun porch to the front yard was never used, but by fiddling with the latch I was eventually able to pull the swollen door open. I escaped down the steps into the yard, where cold raindrops plopped on my face, but they could have been honey, they felt so sweet.

I climbed the trembling, fire-escape stairs to my home. I felt exhausted, drained, but a terrible anger made my chest feel as if it were full of thousands of red ants, scratching, burning, biting. I lay on my bed and cried away my humiliation. Then I set to work.

I already knew how the next episode of *Slugger McBatt* was going to end. It involved the Bat and was titled "Diamond Doom." The Bat had disguised himself and slipped into the stadium. Armed with his deadly Bat Walking Stick, which was really a rifle, he was going to shoot Slugger McBatt in the back as Slugger patrolled right field.

But just as the evil Bat was about to plug our hero, a scorching line drive was hit to deep right field. The Bat, though his heart was filled with evil, was above all else a lover of baseball. No villain, no matter how nefarious, would shoot a player as he was chasing down a line drive.

My plan was for Slugger to make a leaping catch of the liner, almost falling into the stands as he did so. The ball safely in his glove for the third out of the inning, he would recognize his adversary and, with one swift motion, hit the Bat on his pig nose, causing the deadly bat rifle to discharge harmlessly in the air. Slugger would bow modestly to the crowd as his good friend Police Chief Rafferty hauled the Bat off to jail. Slugger would mouth a variation of the "Baseball is a clean and worthwhile sport" line, and the episode would end. I was already creating a villain named the Plate, who would have a pentagonal head and body.

I had outlined the strip on a sheet of box factory cardboard, heading it up "The Further Adventures of Slugger McBatt," and allowing myself twelve squares, three rows of four, to finish the episode.

In the first square I drew the Bat, weapon in hand, peering furtively over the railing of a box seat as the unsuspecting Slugger made his way to right field.

In the second panel the hitter connected with the ball, and it sailed toward right field.

In the third, Slugger, glove held high, was leaping toward the ball, while the announcer's voice cried, "It's a long drive to deep right field. Looks like it's going to land in the bleachers."

In the final panel of the first row, Slugger made the catch and grabbed onto the rail of a box seat to stop his forward motion, coming as he did face to face with the Bat.

In the fifth panel the Bat's infamous Bat Walking Stick went POW! POW! POW! while Slugger, who resembled Freddie more than ever before, stood with a stunned expression on his face.

In the final panel, Slugger lay sprawled on the grass; the side view of his face was Freddie's face contorted in death, blood leaking from the corner of his mouth. The Bat was slinking away into the crowd. The caption read: *Shot through the heart!*

With my red pen I drew beautiful drops of blood, which dripped menacingly into the empty panels below.

Frank Pierce, Iowa

THE NARRATOR of the following story is my friend Marylyle Baron. For several years prior to her death, she imparted to me what I call the Oral History of Johnson County, Iowa. After Marylyle's death in her ninetieth year, I took custody of her daughter, Melissa (Missy), a victim of Down's syndrome. Missy lives with me now in my huge frame house with a wrought-iron widow's walk in the nearby town of Onamata. Missy is beyond middle age and has far outlived her life expectancy. She is a delightful companion, sweet and guileless as a child, always cheerful, a perfect listener.

This story was told to me in the kitchen of Marylyle's farmhouse, a mile outside Onamata. Her kitchen always smelled of cinnamon and coffee. She sat across the table from me, her white hair pulled tightly in a bun. We drank coffee, while across the room Missy stroked her orange cat, which was curled into a circular pillow in her lap.

"In 1901 there was a U.S. Post Office in the store at Frank Pierce, Iowa," Marylyle begins. "Zundel's General Store, it was known as. There wasn't much else, a dirt street, a blacksmith shop with a heavy sliding door, a barbershop scarcely the size of a granary, though it had a high false front and a piece of peeled timber painted in circular red, white, and blue stripes attached to the front of the building, just to the right of the door. There were five or six houses, frame or log or a combination of the two, and a one-room school, actually a granary on skids with sod banked about the sides and a window cut into the south side by Jim James, one of two handymen in the town.

"And of course there was the church, the only building in Frank Pierce that had seen paint, other than the false front of the barbershop. Saint Zacharias was only about twenty by twenty and drew its congregation from the farm families, some of whom traveled over five miles by horse and wagon to come to Sunday services.

"When that same group of farm families persuaded the bishop in Des Moines to send them a priest, they promised a manse, but somehow it never got built, and Father Camino, a slim, dark-eyed young priest from New Mexico, boarded with one of the town families for a while, until he decided that if a heater were provided he could live adequately if not comfortably in the back six feet of the church. The area behind the altar was cordoned off with blankets. A heater, a generous supply of wood, a couple of chairs, a bed and bedding, and a bookcase were donated. The priest still took his meals with a town family but was able to spend the remainder of his time in private, away from worldly distractions.

"The story I want to tell you happened on a Sunday morning in August. It was approaching noon. The service at Saint Zacharias had been in progress for nearly an hour. A searing sun burned down from a cloudless sky, the humidity was high, the air like hot flannel. The sun's rays reflected on the yellow dust of the main street with such force that particles seemed to rise in tiny formations like gnats moving lazily over the earth. There was a hint of a breeze but not enough to effect comfort, only to make the heat more noticeable.

"A dozen wagons were parked on the shady side of Saint Zacharias. Harness bells tinkled, wagons creaked and groaned as horses grazed on the long grass next to the white wall.

"Across the street from the church was the baseball diamond. A ragged chicken-wire backstop and one tiny bleacher made of six faded planks were all that distinguished it from vacant land. The field might have been a pasture; it needed mowing badly. The infield was covered in two-inch-high weeds, the outfield grass was bent and cowlicked. There had been heavy rain and no baseball games in Frank Pierce for over two weeks.

"The only people visible in the sunstruck, silent town were two men near the bleacher, one sitting on the third plank up, the other standing on the ground in front of him. The sitting man, Ezra Dean, was the village jack-of-all-trades, and was supposed to have the baseball field mowed, manicured, and ready for a one o'clock game. But his team of horses were still grazing in his back yard a block away, his mower was still idle, grass growing high against the spokes of its wheels. In fact, Ezra had not even honed the blue cutting discs as he would have if he had planned to do the job.

"The standing man was James John James, caretaker of the school, the church (though he was an agnostic and lapsed Protestant), the barbershop, and the general store. Some might have considered him and Ezra rivals, but such was not the case. Each had clearly defined duties. For instance, Jim James did not build cabinets, or dig wells, or do farm work of any kind. Ezra was always available as a temporary hired hand, and was also a veterinarian of sorts, always willing to practice common sense and folk medicine on a sick animal.

" 'I expected to find you riding your mower,' Jim James said to Ezra. 'Maybe even hurrying the horses along so as to create a breeze for comfort.'

"Ezra was a stocky man dressed in heavy work clothes. Railroad suspenders tracked over the shoulders of a collarless ivory shirt. This morning he was barefoot. His hair was dark brown, though his long mustache was the color of brick. He looked at Jim James. With Ezra sitting three rows up and Jim standing, their eyes were virtually level.

" 'It won't be necessary to mow today.'

" 'The game's been canceled?'

" 'It will be. Not canceled. It just won't happen.'

" 'The sky's clear,' said Jim James. 'What do you know that I don't?'

"James John James ran a hand through his thick, sandy hair. He, too, was dressed in work clothes; his boots were handmade of black leather.

" 'The world's about to end,' said Ezra without emotion.

" 'Oh, Ezra, don't tell me one of them pain-pushin' travelin' preachers has got to you.' Jim James shook his head. 'If you'll let me, I'll hitch up your team and mow the baseball field. The players will be mad as wet hens.'

" 'No need.'

" 'Care to explain yourself?'

"From the direction of the outfield, the burble of a meadowlark rose sweet as fresh water. Father Camino's voice droned from the church, harness bells jingled faintly.

" 'I had a dream —' and here Ezra Dean faltered, expecting Jim James to laugh, but he didn't. If there was one thing Jim James knew, it was that Ezra's word was as reliable as sunrise and sunset. If Ezra said the baseball field would be mowed by Sunday noon, then only death or catastrophe would stop him.

" 'And?' said Jim James.

"Beyond the outfield was corn, the tall stalks shimmering like a green ocean beneath the fierce sun. The crop ripening, filling the humid air with the sweet smell of life.

" 'I was visited in my dream by a boy of about ten. He never spoke; he just emerged from the cornfield, right over there, in that spot where the stalks are parted. He was dressed in a suit and tie, a little gentleman. He stared at me with brown eyes filled to overflowing with the most terrible sadness. The voice that spoke to me may have been his voice, but it came from all around me, not just from the boy's mouth.'

" 'We all have strange dreams,' said Jim James. 'You're not alone.'

"A quarter mile deep in the cornfield were the railroad tracks, invisible at that time of year, though both men knew the sun would be glinting shrilly off the silver rails. The railroad had not considered

Frank Pierce, Iowa, important enough for even a whistle stop. Once a day, windowpanes rattled, dishes vibrated, and dogs barked as the train grumbled across the plains. Today, the distant odor of creosote was the only indication that the railroad existed.

" 'I am alone,' said Ezra. 'No one else knows what I know. The church is in session. The world goes on unaware . . .'

"Across the street, a gray hen ruffled her feathers in the yellow dust beside the front porch of a house, clucking occasionally to herself.

" 'The world is ending, then?'

" 'Not the world,' said Ezra Dean. 'No. It is just us who have been called. Frank Pierce, Iowa.'

" 'Not even all of Johnson County?'

" ' Frank Pierce, Iowa,' Ezra reiterated.

" 'If I didn't know you for a truthful man, I'd call you a liar,' said Jim James. 'If I didn't know you as a temperate man, I'd call you a drunk.' He strode a few steps toward home plate and scraped the yellowish dust with his foot. A cloud rose and settled almost instantly on his trousers and boots.

" 'I'm tellin' you only what I know as truth,' said Ezra, examining the toenails on his left foot, painstakingly, as if there might be a message printed on them. 'Our world, this town, will die at noon.'

"James John James pulled on a brown shoelace just below his beltline and extracted a silver pocket watch. Holding it in the palm of his right hand, he studied it, watching the circle at the bottom of the watch face where a second hand jerked like an insect leg.

" 'We'll know soon,' he said. 'What I don't understand is why you think your dream more important than anyone else's? And why, if only Frank Pierce is to cease to exist, don't you run? And why, if you believe your dream is truth, you, who profess to believe in higher powers, stay away from church, and don't even put on your shoes to meet your maker?'

" 'Because I *know* my dream was truth,' said Ezra, speaking with more dignity than he was used to. He had never felt so important. There was no way he could find words to tell Jim James why he would not run, could not run. 'I'm not at all sure that what will happen to us has anything to do with *them*,' he went on, pointing toward Saint Zacharias. 'If you count, you will find not one soul is absent from Frank Pierce today. If you count the wagons by the church you will see that every parishioner of Saint Zacharias is in his pew this morning. I doubt if I, or even an unbeliever like you, could run, though you should feel free to try. If, of course, you believe me. All I know, Jim, is the child of my dreams said to me, "Ezra, tomorrow, when the sun is highest in the noontime sky, you will be set free." '

" 'Was the dream before or after midnight? Perhaps the end spoken of is not due until tomorrow. I think we should cut the grass, just in case.'

" 'I don't blame you for making light of the idea,' Ezra went on. 'But let me tell you the real reason I didn't run. I think it's going to be fun. That little boy, that sad, serious, little boy, said there won't be any pain or misery involved in the passing. We will simply become invisible to all but our own eyes. We will become weightless and no sound will issue from our lips.'

"Jim James again backed up a few steps; he leaned against the edge of the backstop. He produced a pouch of tobacco and papers from a trousers pocket and proceeded to roll a cigarette.

" 'All right,' said Jim James. 'Suppose it is as you say. We make no more sounds. No one outside of Frank Pierce sees us for ought to see. What then?' He struck a blue-headed wooden match on the backstop and cupped his hands around the cigarette, though there was only a hint of a breeze.

" 'Perhaps we drift with the wind, as flower seeds are carried to new beginnings. Who is to say what wonder we will discover when we become aware of what lies invisible about us. Perhaps the air is full of shades. Perhaps there are layers and layers of history living right here, dimension piled upon dimension — the past like curtains hung in rows — like the gauzy greenness of the northern lights. What do you think of that?'

" 'I think the baseball players are gonna be after your hide when church lets out and the grass ain't mowed,' said Jim James, exhaling smoke.

" 'Come on, Jim. How many years have we played ball here on this diamond?'

" 'Before I came to Frank Pierce, twenty years, I suppose.'

" 'Each one of those games is out there like a sweet, shy ghost, waiting to be seen again,' said Ezra.

" 'I don't think I like the gist of your idea. You scare me, Ezra. I don't like what I'm hearin' at all.'

" 'How many times do you reckon this has happened before, Jim? How many times does a town or a county or a section of a city just disappear off the face of the earth, leaving only the land behind, soft and natural and renewed — something man doesn't have sense enough to do himself? Frank Pierce, Iowa, is going to be wiped from memories, easy as cleaning a slate with a damp cloth.'

" 'I think I'll mosey up the road, or maybe I'll cut across the field to the railroad tracks . . .' But Jim James remained immobile, leaning on the unpainted backstop.

"From the church, the small pump organ fired notes into the still noontime air — they seemed to have life. Ezra thought the notes flying from the windows and open door cast flitting shadows on the earth. He thought he saw the notes rise through the roof like heat, then evaporate like steam into the pale sky.

" 'Think of it, Jim. We'll be free of the weight that binds us to the earth. We'll soar with the wind like the leaves of the autumn, we'll soar like music. Instead of being the baseball players, we'll be the ball, the bat, the bases. Adventure like we've never known — I rode with Teddy Roosevelt in . . . what was the year? It will be even greater than that.'

"Jim James had seized the wire of the backstop with one hand. Though the wire was cutting into his fingers, he seemed intent only on holding onto something tangible.

" 'I think I know now why I've been entrusted with this secret,' said Ezra Dean, suddenly rising, stepping down from the bleacher, and walking toward his friend. 'I am not afraid, yet I know there will be many who won't understand, who will need comfort.'

"Ezra Dean opened his arms toward the high, clear, noontime sky.

" 'I wish only to drift on the earth, and then only from Frank Pierce to places where my legs can safely return me,' said Jim James, drawing deeply on his cigarette.

" 'I'll help you to adjust, my friend,' said Ezra. 'What is about to happen to us will not be death.' Here Ezra clamped a hand firmly on Jim's shoulder. 'But if you are so afraid, there is still time. Run, my friend. Run through the corn like a fielder chasing the ultimate fly ball. Run like your life depends on it.'

" 'I can't,' said Jim James. 'I can't.' He gripped the mesh of the backstop more fiercely.

" 'I know,' said Ezra. 'Look!' He pointed across the baseball diamond. Emerging from the rows of tall, fertile corn was the boy, a well-dressed young man of about ten, with hair parted in the middle and brushed into place. As the two men stood side by side on the baseball field, the boy advanced slowly, solemnly, toward them.

" 'Feel the total silence that falls about us now,' whispered Ezra, for the organ had become silent, Father Camino's voice still. The silence became more pronounced, the buzz of a distant bee, the twitter of birds, the tremble of harness bells, the groan of horseflesh, all ceased.

" 'It's our imagination,' said Jim James. His whisper sounded like a shout. 'The voices from the church stop only for silent prayer.' He made no effort to remove his friend's hand from his shoulder. 'The silence is always here in the heat. A breeze, I felt a breeze on my face. How do you explain . . .'

"The words died on the lips of James John James. He talked on, though no sound issued from his mouth. He gestured with his free hand. He looked with alarm at his shoulder, where Ezra's hand still rested. Jim James could not feel that hand. He reached out to touch Ezra, but his hand passed through empty space.

"The boy, dark-eyed and solemn, was near to the pitcher's mound now, walking steadily, mechanically, when suddenly he did a back flip, a graceful, ballet-like movement. Landing on his feet, his expression changed to a smile so angelic, so full of release, that both men found themselves smiling and taking a step or two toward the child.

"Though he knew that sound had ceased, Jim James thought he heard the bright, energetic chatter of baseball players, the crack of hickory on horsehide, the murmur of spectators. He thought he could detect player shapes at or near each position, but faint and fleeting, like a passing reflection on a window.

"The boy was laughing now, tossing a ball in his pudgy hands. The searing heat still reigned. That angel's breath of a breeze moved the bleacher, the backstop, the church, the people who were emerging from the church, staring around trying to understand — moved them all gently as dust demons move over hardwood.

"Ezra Dean flapped his arms, rose a few feet in the air, drifted easy as a leaf floating down from a tree. He turned a cartwheel, landed beside the smiling child, who flipped the ball to him underhanded. Ezra caught it and dipped toward second base as if tagging a sliding runner.

"Ezra waved at James John James, and his mouth formed words, though no sound issued forth: 'Look at me, Jim. Look at me; I fly with the wind like the leaves of the autumn.'"

Marylyle's story ends with the town of Frank Pierce, Iowa, disappearing like Brigadoon into the haze of a sultry summer noon, on an August Sunday in 1901. All that was left was the tall, ripening corn; the only sounds came from outside the immediate area of the town: a few bird chirps, the drone of a bee, the eerie rustling of the green corn.

Such events were accepted in the early days of Johnson County, a time when the presence of magic was taken for granted. Marylyle's favorite expression was, "Things are out of kilter in Johnson County." And indeed, up to and including the present day, they are.

What Marylyle didn't include, perhaps didn't know, though I'm more inclined to think she forgot, or for some reason didn't think it important to the story, was some comment on the name of the town. Surely she knew that Frank Pierce, Iowa, was named for Franklin Pierce, fourteenth president of the United States, 1853 to 1856.

Why would a hamlet in eastern Iowa be named for an unmemorable former president some fifty years after his term of office had expired? Some of the early settlers must have known the story of how, immediately after his election in 1852 (he would not be inaugurated until March of 1853), Frank Pierce set out for Kansas on a peacemaking mission, trying to win over the strong secessionist element in the Sunflower State. On his way there, somewhere in Iowa, old newspapers establish only that in a desolate area of rolling plains and cornfields, some miles east of Des Moines, there was a train wreck. It was probably sabotage, though no clear conclusions were ever reached. President Pierce was not hurt, but to his horror, his only surviving child, an eleven-year-old son, was crushed to death in front of his eyes. Even on inauguration day, President Pierce was still in a state of emotional collapse.

Where did Marylyle Baron hear the story of the disappearance of Frank Pierce, Iowa? I did not ask her sources for fear of drying up the supply. But there was a Frank Pierce, Iowa. If you consult the list of Abandoned Post Offices in the archives of the University of Iowa library in Iowa City, you find that the Frank Pierce Post Office came into being in 1895 and was abandoned in 1901. Some post offices were absorbed by larger ones, some simply discontinued because of shifts in population. On the line beneath "Reasons for Abandonment," beside the name Frank Pierce, is the single word, "Unknown."

K Mart

For Lesley Choyce

"THE PAST is so melodramatic," my wife said to me not long ago. "I remember standing at the sink with a plate raised over my head," she went on, "screaming at my first husband, bringing the plate down on the pile of broken dishes already in the sink, screaming louder. I don't even remember what I was mad about. I've never done anything like that since we've been married. But then you don't goad me. I keep remembering all those terrible life-and-death situations when I was a teenager; you must have suffered the same kind: she loves me, she loves me not. If he doesn't ask me out I'll die. None of them were ever as disastrous as I feared they would be."

"Some are," I said.

"Name one," she said.

"Well . . ." I said and remained silent, smiling wryly, letting her think she had me. But I was thinking of Cory.

"If we lived in the South we'd be white trash," my mother said as she stared around the living room of the dark, dilapidated house we were moving into. I was not quite fourteen and had spent all my life in a dreamy, small town called Onamata on the banks of the Iowa River, until suddenly, the hardware store my father had inherited from his father failed, and our big, old house with its wide verandahs and creaking porch swing was sold to pay off creditors.

We were not in the South but on the outskirts of a dingy factory town in Illinois, where a never-before-seen relative had found my father a job as a nighttime security guard at a tool and die plant.

There were dust demons on the scuffed floorboards. The previous tenants had left behind the skeleton of a chrome kitchen chair, scabby food particles dried on the legs. The chair glinted sickly under a single pale light bulb. We were, in my mother's no-nonsense way of speaking, "making the best of a bad situation." The year was 1949.

The cast of characters: Bronislaw Kazimericz, Edward Kleinrath, Corrina Mazeppa, and a character named Jamie (Flash) Kirkendahl who, when I look back, is less real to me than many of my fictional creations. The nickname, incidentally, was an irony, tacked to me because of my lack of speed on the basepaths, perpetuated because of my propensity to fall down while trying to get out of the batter's box after hitting the ball. Jamie Kirkendahl would say this is not a story about baseball. Perhaps I should let you be the judge of that.

"What are you lookin' at, Stretch?" were the first words Bronislaw Kazimericz ever said to me. It was noon hour on my first day at a cinder block school that looked more like a factory or a prison.

I hadn't been looking at anything. In fact I had been standing alone alongside a chain link fence wishing I was almost anywhere else. I looked at the speaker, a squat, blond boy, heavily muscled. He had a wide, pink face, pale blue eyes, and a soft, flat nose like a baby's.

"Kaz beats up every new kid, just to show who's boss of the playground," said a thin boy with the face of a weasel, Coke-bottle glasses, and a shoelace of mud-colored hair that fell down on his forehead as fast as he flicked it back into place.

"So go ahead," I said, making no effort to defend myself.

"Aren't you afraid?" said the weasel. "Kaz is the toughest guy in Northside." Northside was both the name of the school and the district within the city where we lived.

"I guess I'm afraid," I said.

"You don't know?"

"If you bruise me or break something it will hurt and maybe I'll forget how miserable I am," I said. "Do your worst."

"Kaz doesn't usually beat up guys unless they want to take him on, or unless they try to get away," said the weasel.

"Shut up, Eddie," said Kaz. "You too good for us, or what?" Kaz said to me.

"If you're gonna kill me, get it over with," I said.

"Go ahead, kill him," said Eddie the weasel.

"I never met one like you," said Kaz. "You got a name?"

"Jamie," I told him.

"I'm Kaz; he's Eddie."

"His real name's Bronislaw," said Eddie, dancing backward in front of Kaz, staying well out of his reach.

"Let only fear and common sense stop *you* from calling me anything but Kaz," he said to me. "By the way, do you play baseball?"

"Yeah, I do," I said.

"Right after school," said Kaz. "Kitty-corner from the back door of the Railroad Hotel," he added, pointing across the gray schoolyard to where, a couple of blocks away, the hotel rose up rectangular and ugly. It was the only building over two stories for blocks.

"Bring your own glove," said Eddie.

I showed up at the baseball field. Baseball was my salvation, for it was the only real connection between my past and present. The game we played here in this dismal factory town with its constantly gray skies was exactly the same game I had played in the sweet, green warmth of an Iowa summer. Here, it was April and the snow was barely gone. If I looked closely I could just make out the fine green tendrils emerging from the earth beneath the brown fuzz of winterkilled grass.

There were some two dozen neighborhood boys from twelve to seventeen who played baseball from the time school was let out until dark, and all day Saturday and Sunday. In that strange way boys have of forming instant alliances, I was accepted by Kaz and Eddie, and because of that was grudgingly accepted by everyone else. Kaz cleared the way for me like a snowplow, for he was indeed a fighter to be reckoned with. He had been Eddie's protector, and now he was mine as well. By the end of the summer it was as if I had lived all my life in Northside. But buried deep within me were memories of a better place and better times and a determination to succeed at *something*. I hated the overcrowded, inferior school, the gritty rows of bars along Railroad Avenue, the meanness, the poverty, the myopia of almost everyone trapped in a hopeless cycle, dependent on the availability of work at the ugly factories. The most important thing in every adult's life was who was hiring workers and who was laying them off.

What did baseball mean to us? Why the daily ritual, the dawn to dusk devotion? We were not good at the game. Kaz could hit the ball a mile, but a good pitcher could make him look ridiculous. I was a sneaky hitter; I held out my bat and let the ball do the work. I hit dying quail Texas Leaguers to all fields. I was the only one who kept meticulous records of my batting average. My on-base percentage was over .560, but in a game where power hitting was everything, I was one of the least valuable players. Eddie had virtually no skills at all; his poor eyesight made him a liability both at bat and in the field, but he was never picked last because if Kaz wasn't a captain, he insisted that whoever picked him had to make Eddie their next pick.

Baseball held us together like glue. Kaz, Eddie, and I became known as the Three K's, because each of us had a long, difficult name beginning with that letter. In science we had studied simple chemical compounds, and the diagrams of those compounds, dots joined by dark lines until they looked like constellations of stars, reminded me of our own attachments, and of the endless combinations we formed each day as the pickup game went on.

It was during that first summer in Northside that I met Cory Mazeppa, the fourth major character in this story, the pivotal character. If it wasn't for Cory, there would be no story. Her family operated a small grocery store across the street from the baseball field. We were in and out of the store two or three times a day all summer, and when she didn't have to work behind the counter, Cory would wander across Railroad Avenue and sit along one sideline or another watching the baseball game. She was a year younger but two grades behind me in school.

Mazeppa, Kaz informed me, was a Mongol name; he claimed there was some famous Mongol leader named Mazeppa. I often intended to look for confirmation in history books, but never have. The family claimed to be Yugoslavs who had crossed the border from Italy a century before. The parents had immigrated to America just before the Second World War. Cory would tell me a year later that she was conceived in the old country, born in the U.S.A. They belonged to a European church of some kind. It was housed in a sturdy building with a white steeple, formerly occupied by Lutherans who sold it after they built a flat, single-story church covered in yellow California stucco. The signboard outside Mazeppas' church was covered in upside-down writing that Kaz said was Russian. At least four gaunt, bearded, and black-cassocked clergymen lived in the church basement, and could occasionally be seen walking single file, hands behind their back, down Railroad Avenue.

I would see the family file out the rear door of the small residence attached to the Mazeppa Family Grocery and head off in the direction of their church: the parents, Cory, her sisters, Mary and Pauline, one older, one younger, and a brother of about five who was always dressed in a replica of an adult suit and a tweed cap. The girls often wore billowing skirts and peasant blouses with brilliant embroidery patterns in vermilion, aquamarine, and kelly green.

Cory had soft brown eyes, chocolate hair, and a scattering of freckles across her cheeks and nose. She was shy and tended to look away if one of us tried to make eye contact with her at the baseball field. We were braver at the store and would tease her and try to confuse her change-making. None of us admitted any interest in girls that first summer, though I used to daydream of Cory when I came to bat, fantasizing myself in the big leagues, Cory my faithful sweetheart gallantly cheering me on against impossible odds. If I hit, I looked to where she sat, her skirt a tent floating about her on the grass. I was hoping for recognition, praise, a sign, knowing that if she did acknowledge me I would be the subject of unmerciful teasing, but I didn't care.

Baseball inextricably ties the four main characters together. But, as I've said, Cory is the important one, the fourth character. If Cory hadn't died there wouldn't be a story. But Cory chose to act, to end her life. If she had chosen not to act, to instead live out her days in the stifling cookie-cutter apartment, one in a complex of 250 identical apartments on the outskirts of Northside, apartments with gray stucco exteriors and close, airless interiors; if she had chosen to live that way, abandoned with her brood of children, she would have become only a passing memory to the Three K's. To Kirkendahl she would have been a warm, grayish memory that would flit to the surface of consciousness every year or so on a honeysuckle-sweet summer evening, when fireflies glittered like sequins in the soft darkness. And she would have been even less to the other two.

But she did act, in her thirtieth year. Just as by thirty each of the others had acted. Kirkendahl quit his job as a sportswriter and lived off his wife's income while he researched and wrote *Murder's Blue Gown*, the re-creation of a sensational crime that had rocked a nearby Illinois industrial suburb. The book had sex, mystery, and mutilation. It eventually sold eighty thousand copies and was made into a B movie starring Dean Stockwell that still turns up occasionally on the late, late show. The income from the book and movie allowed the author to pursue a full-time writing career. Kazimericz turned one used gravel truck into a small empire, then married into money.

Kleinrath discovered his religious heritage. And Cory Mazeppa committed suicide.

My father was a confused, unhappy man, supervised by my mother. He had served as a medic in World War I, and his superiors told him he had the skill and temperament to be a doctor. But instead of becoming a doctor he did what was expected of him and returned to Iowa and the family hardware store.

"Don't ever let anyone talk you out of being what you want to be," he told me on more than one occasion. That was about the only advice he ever gave me, for we were awkward around each other, our time together full of clumsy silences. Father was pale and thin with a fringe of blondish hair. He spent his life doing a job he hated while Mother hovered behind him, bullying and cajoling. Grandfather, who retired to California, still sent long detailed letters in his large, vertical hand, offering advice, no, giving instruction, on pricing, inventory, and promotion. But Father had the last laugh, and I will always have a soft spot in my heart for him because of it. In spite of everyone's good intentions he managed to stay drunk on the contents of nefariously hidden bottles of vodka for over twenty years. He also flimflammed the books so my mother never suspected the insolvency of the business until the bankers arrived, padlocks in hand, to close the store. My Father continued to drink; he would set off for his job as a security guard armed with a fifth of vodka and a heavy copy of *Gray's Anatomy*.

For all our bad times, we were better off than my friends. We had, if not a happy family, at least a relatively tranquil one. My mother would hiss at my father only long after I was in bed, supposedly asleep. I never heard exactly what she said, but I know my father never defended himself against whatever charges she made.

The time she made the remark about us being white trash my mother was about as depressed as she ever got. She rallied quickly and fixed up the house. She sewed bright curtains, scrubbed every inch of the place with Lysol, planted an extravaganza of flowers in the ugly front yard: poppies, pansies, heavy-headed white mums, sweet peas, cosmos, and hollyhocks. My bedroom reminded me of a coffin; my single bed filled the room. Mother put up a shelf alongside the bed and tacked a curtain to it to separate me from the bluish mildew that covered the wall.

She also made some quick alliances in the neighborhood: a Mrs. Piska, a Mrs. Hlushak, a Mrs. Hearne. "Misery loves company," she loved to say. The four of them would congregate for coffee each morning at the oilcloth-covered table in one of their kitchens. Mrs. Piska was roly-poly and always wore a black babushka festooned with blood-colored roses; she rolled her own fat cigarettes and in her heavy Polish accent stated that even though she had been married for over thirty years, her husband, Bronko, did not know she smoked. Mrs. Hlushak's only son was in jail for car theft; Mrs. Hearne, who had nine children, carried religious medals in her apron pocket and often gave the other ladies one when the coffee klatch broke up.

We at least had running water. Kaz lived in a cluster of shacks that didn't even have the dignity of being assigned a street address. His mother was dead; his father was a brutish drunk; he had one sister of about eleven who grew wild and untended. Kaz's father worked from four to midnight at the Firestone Tire plant. After work he would stop at one of the all-night bars along Railroad Avenue, drink himself into a rage, fistfight with whoever was handy, and often end up sprawled on the gravel behind the hotel. On more than one occasion I slipped out of the house deep in the night after Kaz tapped on the wall behind my head (my room had no window), and the two of us took turns pulling Kaz's metal wagon home from the hotel, his father face down, mumbling, cursing, his hands dragging on the street.

Eddie was the third of four children. His family lived in a shack with a slanted roof, and they had to carry water from a community water spigot four blocks away. Eddie's father, Isaac Kleinrath, claimed they were Hungarian Gypsies. Eddie said they were Jewish and called his father "The Rabbi" behind his back.

*

I don't think anyone ever realizes the best times of their lives while those times are happening. It's just as well, for if they did, they would realize that everything else is downhill, no matter how gentle and gradual the slope, and they would stop trying, stop striving. I suppose it was sometime in my twenties when I realized that my *baseball days,* those three summers I spent in Northside, had so far been the best days of my life. That time when baseball was like the sun lighting my days. I was through university, working my way up the ranks in the newspaper business, ambitious, acquisitive, when the first suspicions appeared. My suspicions, shadows, gray, disturbing, like animals skulking about the edge of a camp, came in the form of disturbing thoughts about Cory, mixed with pleasant reveries about baseball. I dreamed of the long, sunny afternoons on the field where our endless game went on from the time the dew left the grass until it was too dark to see the ball. We played a game called Eleven, where if either team was ahead by eleven or more runs after even innings the game was called; we either started over or broke up and chose new sides. I can still hear Eddie's shrill "Way to go, Flash," as I ran in on a fly ball that was going yards over my head, or as I crashed to the ground after connecting with the ball, taking precious seconds to get to my feet, turning a double into a single.

I loved those times, the tense, uncaring heat of August, the air thick, sweat drizzling into my eyebrows. I remember grabbing the bottom of my damp T-shirt, pulling it up and wiping my forehead, drying my eyes before heading for the plate. I remember squinting through a haze of perspiration from my spot in right field, the earth aerated by cheeky prairie dogs who peeked and chittered all the long, lazy afternoons.

I had been in the enclosed yard behind Mazeppas' store on more than one occasion. In that way boys have of exploring like animals, I had peeked through the caragana hedge, crossed the yard, peered through the window of the garage where Mr. Mazeppa stored a seldom used, pre-war Essex. The car was tan, all square angles, with a windshield that tilted forward. One day I helped Mr. Mazeppa, a grumpy man with a sharp tongue, unload boxes of groceries he had carried home from the wholesaler. I carried in crates of tin cans, boxes full of pungent coffee and exotic-smelling spices. The cottonwood trees were tall with broad leaves. The leaves deflected the sun even in midafternoon, so only a few white diamonds of light would dance on the spongy earth of the yard. A few bluebells grew in the mossy turf, a cool aster bloomed, its purple head bowed by the weight of its lush petals.

One afternoon, a skyful of black clouds stampeded in from the west, bringing heavy wind and rain with them. The game broke up quickly, some players running for home, some seeking shelter nearby. Cory had been sitting on the sidelines alone, as she almost always was; we both ran across the street, dodging the penny-sized raindrops.

"Come on in the yard," she said. I was planning to make a run for home, but I quickly took her up on her invitation. Cory was wearing a mauve dress, a hand-me-down of some kind, that clung to her body. We stood under the leaves for a moment or two. The wind whirled through the tops of the cottonwoods. The tempo of the rain increased but the yard remained dry.

"Do you want to see my rabbit?" Cory asked.

The storm made the yard darker than twilight. We peered through the wire mesh but all we could see were the rabbit's eyes, a phosphorescent amber in a far corner. I touched Cory's hand and my heart bumped as if I'd tripped and stumbled. But I didn't let go. The feeling I experienced was the most beautiful I'd ever known. Being an only child, I had never felt protective toward anyone. It never occurred to me that what I was feeling was sexual, though I considered kissing Cory as we walked slowly to the center of the yard and sat side by side on one of the gnarled roots of the largest cottonwood. Cory's fingers were slim and her hand so much smaller than mine. I couldn't speak, but I glanced at her. Her long hair was uncombed. There were water marks on her cheeks as if she might have cried earlier in the day. I let my arm circle her shoulder, my fingers barely touching the skin of her upper arm. Cory let her head lean against my shoulder. I was just about to turn to kiss her when I glanced down. Below our feet, in the bare dirt near the roots was a scuffle of twigs, feathers, and blood, where a small bird had probably fallen victim to a cat; there was a worm of entrails, an inch of pale yellow, scaly leg.

"What is it?" whispered Cory. I tightened my grip on her shoulder so she wouldn't look down. We were suddenly interrupted by pounding footsteps and loud voices. By the time Kaz and Eddie pushed through the hedge into the tranquillity of the yard, shaking themselves like dogs, Cory and I were sitting a couple of feet apart.

In the spring of my third and final year in Northside, on the opening day of the baseball season, my father died. In his typical way, not wanting to disturb anyone, he died in his sleep. Since he worked nights, it was midafternoon when my mother discovered his body. By the time I got home from school the undertaker had already removed the corpse, funeral arrangements had been made, she had called his employer to say he wouldn't be in again, and had contacted a branch of the insurance company which insured his life. Mother was so efficient that we were hardly inconvenienced at all.

Four months after my father's death, my mother married a man named Nick Walczak, a fifty-two-year-old dairy farmer, and we moved to Wisconsin in time for me to start school in September. Nick was a widower with a grown family. He wore a felt hat and a shiny blue serge suit. His face was windburned and he smelled of cattle. I hated Nick, the farm, Wisconsin, and the Bible Belt high school I attended in a holier-than-thou town called St. Edward. I have to admit that Nick was a good deal more tolerant of me than I would have been of him if our roles had been reversed.

My mother must have met Nick through the personal ads in our daily newspaper, or through a lonely-hearts club of some kind. I imagined his ad: Gent. 52, widower, farmer of some means, seeks marriage-minded woman. Box — — —.

"You're going to become Polish by marriage," Kaz teased me.

Nick claimed to be Estonian but Kaz taught me the vilest Polish curses he knew and Nick seemed to understand them. Someday I am going to write a novel about the year I spent on Nick Walczak's farm in America's Dairyland.

Cory is dead and her death stays with me, a stain on the canvas of my life. When I was a kid in Iowa, in our dark and unused parlor hung a watercolor painted from a photograph, a picture of my mother's older brother. It was a large head-and-shoulders view of what could have been either a boy or a girl: a pink-faced child with rouge cheeks and artificially blue eyes, staring sullenly from a mop of long, blond hair. Charlie had died at age seven from a bee sting to the eye. My mother, a year younger than Charlie, had been playing with him in the garden on a sunstruck afternoon when Charlie bent a tall hollyhock down to his face and the resident bee panicked and stung him on the eyelid. The poison went to his brain and he died a day later.

My mother, in one of the rare moments when she talked about her past, said that she blamed herself for Charlie's death, and that throughout the rest of her childhood she planned how, as soon as she was old enough, she would get pregnant and present her parents with a baby to replace Charlie. "I thought about it endlessly, but I never acted," she said. She was in her mid-thirties when I was born, and by that time both her parents were dead.

There is an Indian legend called "The Woman on the Rocks," and I can't help but recall it as I think of Cory and all the what-might-have-beens. The legend states that young warriors of pure spirit will, as they wander the forests, one day see a beautiful young woman sitting amid rocks at the top of a fearsome waterfall. The girl sees them, beckons to them seductively from behind the white spume of the falls. Each warrior who sees the young woman is immediately captivated, but each, for whatever reason, considers too long before going to her aid. Each one hesitates for a fraction of a second, taking his eyes from the beautiful face for an instant, and when he looks back the maiden on the rocks is gone, swept away to her death perhaps, or simply vanished because of the warrior's indecision. But the warrior is left forever with a memory pure and fresh, cut into his heart — a memory of what might have been if he had been quicker to act. No warrior ever reached the woman on the rocks. Elders interpreted the phenomenon as a moral statement, a truth. Carrying the leaden ball of what-might-have-been deep within us is not a punishment but a lesson. And the ache is not always unpleasant, but often warm and nostalgic, reeking of lost innocence.

But what of the woman on the rocks herself? What happens when she is not a spirit, a lesson, an abstraction, but real flesh and blood with a heart that breaks and a soul full of human longings?

I have tried on several occasions to write about Cory and how she touched my life. About ten years ago I got several pages into a story called "Who Can Eat a Gingerbread Man?" which was about Cory's last hours of life. But I was still too close to the material. I wrote a story about the Three K's, called "Tough Guys." It is one of my few unpublished stories. What follows is the opening page of "Who Can Eat a Gingerbread Man?"

> On a dismal afternoon in February 1967, Corrina Ann Mazeppa (her married name had been Kliciak, but she had taken back her maiden name after the divorce) bundled her three youngest children into their snowsuits, put them into a cab, gave the driver her last ten dollars and her mother's address, telling him to be certain and send the change in with the oldest child.
>
> Corrina Ann Mazeppa, Cory to everyone, closed the door, shivered away the cold draft that had chilled her feet and ankles. She took a last look at the buried yard where snow sculptures like whitecaps sat stiffly in the sullen cold of midwinter. Cory made her way to the bathroom, where cheap plastic curtains covered the frosted glass of the single window. The room smelled of diapers, baby powder, and sour towels. She ran water into the scummy, avocado tub, took off her jeans and sweatshirt, slipped down into the very hot water. She picked up a safety razor, released the blade, rinsed dried soap and hairs from both edges, drew the blade harshly across the underside of her left wrist, changed hands, and cut her right wrist in the same manner. She slid deeper into the water until it touched the back of her neck. Suppressing an urge to vomit, she watched transfixed as her blood colored the water.

I abandoned that fiction, or *faction*. For though we know Cory put her kids in a taxi and later cut her wrists in the bathtub, no one can ever know her thoughts in those last moments.

I remember noticing, those first summers in Northside, how many of the boys at sixteen or seventeen suddenly began drifting away from the eternal pickup game. I couldn't imagine it ever happening to me. But during my final summer, after my father's death, life began interfering with baseball. I got a paper route; for six days a week, from three to six in the afternoon, I had to abandon the game. I also had to miss Friday evenings, which was collection time.

Kaz, the first of us to turn sixteen, got his driver's license and suddenly became obsessed with rebuilding a rusty skeleton of a one-ton truck that had languished in his father's yard for years.

Eddie, the most fearless and outgoing of our group, developed an interest in religion; he visited one of the two synagogues in the city to discuss his Jewishness.

"You circumsized?" he asked me one day as we slouched along Railroad Avenue.

"No," I replied.

"At the synagogue they asked me and I told them the truth. I wish I'd lied. I wonder if they really check your dong to make sure you've been cut?"

"I wouldn't know," I said.

And of course we all discovered girls. Some of us more than others. I was one of the others. Most of the girls I knew were shrill, giggling brats. Kaz suddenly started talking about one or two of the older girls who were reputed to put out; he talked as if he was speaking from experience. Eddie emulated Kaz, though I had more doubts about his claims. "What about you?" Kaz said one evening. "You're not cherry, are you?"

"I know my way around," I said defensively.

But Eddie was the one who talked, about anybody and everybody. "Oh, God," he'd cry as we walked away from Mazeppas' store in the twilight. "Did you see the knockers under that sweater of Cory's?

I'd sell my right nut just to touch them. One touch and I'd die happy." He would fumble through his jacket pockets looking for matches to light his cigarette, his eyes bleary slits behind his thick glasses.

I was surprised one night when Kaz called Eddie on his wishful thinking. "You're all talk, Kleinrath," he said. "You're talking about Cory Mazeppa, for chrissakes. Anybody can do it with Cory."

Kleinrath was all ears and I, too, was silent as Kaz told us how Cory had taken him into the back seat of the square-fendered Essex. I knew Cory didn't come to the ballfield very often anymore. I'd seen her walking with a boy named Buck Johnson; he was white trash, a pock-faced kid who worked on the killing floor of the packing plant. He had a long, equine head and a greasy pompadour. Another time I saw her duck into her yard with Nick Kliciak, a thug who lived at the Passtime Pool Hall. He was short, and, even though he was only a year or two older than us, wore a charcoal-gray suit and pink shirt with an inch-wide black tie.

A week later, Eddie was echoing Kaz's story word for word.

"Come on, Kirkendahl," he said, "get in on the act. You've always had a thing for Cory, haven't you?"

I only smiled and changed the subject.

This is not one of those heartwarming stories of lasting friendships and lifelong loyalties. After I left Northside, we did not stay in touch. I finished high school in Wisconsin, moved to the warmth of California, and married a California girl. Now I seldom leave the state except to go on book promotion tours, which was what brought me to Illinois in the winter of 1967.

A few years after we left Northside, after my mother had been widowed for a second time — this time being left well off financially — she did a very strange thing. She moved back to Northside. She rented a modest apartment on the edge of the old neighborhood, and took up where she had left off with her old friends. The four of them have all been widowed for years and years. Among them they have the complete oral history of Northside in their heads. My mother can recite from memory the history of all the families who populated the district when we first moved there thirty-five years ago.

"You remember Heather Bratus," she'll write to me. "She married the youngest Dzuba boy, from the packing-plant Dzubas, not the lumber-yard Dzubas — well, her daughter . . ." She will tell me a long, often pointless, story about someone I know only by name. I often remind her that I lived only about three years in Northside, but she can't seem to comprehend that, at least for more than a few minutes.

But it was through my mother that I knew what became of Kaz, Eddie, and Cory.

"Eddie, that nice boy with the bad eyesight, is an architect now. He turned Jewish. But then his name always was, wasn't it? He married the daughter of the founder of the firm he works for." She even went so far as to clip the bold-type listing from an outdated Yellow Pages directory: MOSER, SALTZMAN, GREEN & KLEINRATH, followed by a prestigious address in the downtown area of the city.

"Your friend Bronislaw is a millionaire," my mother reported. "Mrs. Piska says he owns a thousand trucks. But no one can figure how he got his money. Mrs. Hearne says he was doing something illegal to start with, drugs or stolen goods . . ." Kaz as Gatsby. Interesting. I've seen Kaz's trucks in southern California, golden transports and tankers, with Bronze Transport in swirling script on the doors and down each side, a small Polish flag beneath the curlicued *B* in Bronze. "Your friend Bronislaw married the ex-mayor's daughter. I guess two fortunes are better than one."

Once she mentioned Cory. "Pauline, the youngest Mazeppa girl — you remember the family has that little store on Railroad Avenue — got married over the weekend to a mining engineer from Chicago. A big splash at the Russian Orthodox Church and a huge reception at Northside Community Hall. I hope she's done better than the middle girl; she married one of the awful Kliciak boys and has had nothing but grief."

*

As my final summer in Northside moved into the heat of July, I found myself doing what I vowed I'd never do. I drifted further and further away from the continuous baseball game. My paper route took up my time; I had money to spend. I helped Kaz work on his truck. He taught me to drive.

One evening, as I headed home from Kaz's place, I found myself crossing the baseball field at twilight. There had been a heavy thunderstorm an hour or two before and the game hadn't resumed. The grass was sopping, the air fresh as an April morning. As I neared home plate, I saw someone leaning against the backstop.

The last red tines of sunset clawed across the field. I recognized Cory by her silhouette. She beckoned to me. I walked slowly toward her across the damp infield. She smiled shyly. "It's so fresh out here," she said. "I like the air after a storm." I didn't say anything. "You haven't been around very much this summer," she went on. I mumbled about being busy, about working on Kaz's truck. I became conscious that though I'd washed my hands I still smelled like solvent and had more grease on my clothes than I was comfortable with.

Cory didn't seem to notice. "Let's walk," she said. And she took my hand as if it were the most natural thing in the world for her to do.

"Pickup! Pickup!" screamed a couple of shrill voices from across Railroad Avenue as we started up the wooden sidewalk toward the edge of town. Though the words were directed at Cory, the girls yelling were schoolmates of mine, Ruthie Fontana and Cookie Brost. I realize now that Cory was doing what they didn't have the nerve to do. But what she was doing made her different, and there is no room anywhere for people who are different. "Pickup!" they screamed again, then went into a fit of shrill giggling.

"Don't pay any attention," whispered Cory.

Cory's father had made her quit school on her fifteenth birthday. For nearly a year, her life had revolved around the dark little store that smelled of coffee and oily floorboards. I didn't speak but I squeezed Cory's hand in a gesture of reassurance. I thought of

Ruthie Fontana, pale, hatchet-faced, eyes quick as a bird's. Ruthie went steady with one of the Bjarnson boys, who lived down by the stockyards. They had a blanket stashed in the bushes behind a Coppertone sign way out at the end of Railroad Avenue; they went there every day after school and had probably spent half the summer there, too. But they were going steady.

There I was, walking up the sidewalk, the first hints of ground mist rising from the grassy gutters. Me, the clutch hitter, heart thrumming, tongue clotted in my mouth because I was holding the hand of a girl I'd known for three years and seen every baseball summer day that whole time.

We slowed and stepped into a gateway where tall, yellow caragana rose high above our heads. Cory turned to face me. I held her, my hands flat on the middle of her back, and we kissed. Cory was soft in my arms and she smelled sweet; her lipstick was slick against my lips. We clung that way for a long time. I remained totally silent. I kissed down the side of her face, across her cheek and back to her lips. They parted willingly. At the same time, I was as happy and as frightened as I had ever been in my life. Cory needed to be held. So did I. Fantasies of rescue flashed through my mind. Cory moved one hand to the back of my neck, twined her fingers in my hair, pulled my face closer to hers. She had none of the coyness of the girls I went to school with, girls who doled out half-returned kisses for favors real or imagined.

We walked on slowly, our arms now twined around each other's waists. The only sound was our shoes on the hollow wooden sidewalk. The sidewalk ended a block farther on. A single avocado-green house sat fifty yards back from the street, a cow grazing near it. In the distance a dog yapped.

We sat on the end of the sidewalk and kissed some more. Cory swung both her legs over my closest one. One of my arms braced her back. I kept thinking of what Eddie and Kaz said about her, of my seeing her with Nick Kliciak. What was expected of me? Wasn't instinct supposed to play some part in a situation like this? Wasn't I supposed to know what to do? I had no idea what to do. Cory was wearing a soft, pink sweater and a brown skirt. Her dark hair was restrained by pink barrettes shaped like kittens. I tentatively touched the sweater, let my fingers slide across to her breast. Cory didn't resist, so I cupped her breast gently, trying to convey affection through my touch. My throat felt cemented shut, like a useless plumbing pipe. I could say nothing. I tried once to speak her name, just her name, a whisper in a tone that would convey some feeling. What emerged was a helpless sound, like a shoe being extracted from mud.

"Your arm is shaking," Cory said, burying her face in my neck. My left arm, which supported her back, was trembling.

"I'm all right," I managed. Cory shifted her weight, wrapped her arms tightly around my neck, kissed me fiercely. I caressed her breast.

"Please, please, please," Cory murmured, holding on to me so hard her own arms trembled. We sat for several more minutes, kissing, touching gently.

"I have to get back," Cory said finally. "Papa will miss me." We walked back toward the lights of Northside, our arms still twined around each other's waists.

When we got to her door I cleared my throat and said, "Thanks, Cory." I felt like a fool the instant the words were out.

"For what?" She smiled, I think sadly, stood on her tiptoes, and brushed her lips across mine. "Do you like me?" she said suddenly, slipping her arms around me, resting her head against my chest.

"Yes, I really like you," I said.

"Will you come by tomorrow evening?"

"I will. I promise."

Cory slipped away, closing the screen door softly behind her.

My wife and I sometimes work as a team on journalistic assignments. She does the interviewing; I do the writing. I don't like interviewing people, because silence is still a problem in my life. Weeks after an interview I think of all the questions I should have asked. I relive the interview again and again even though it is water under the bridge. In the same manner I have spent a great deal of my life thinking about Cory. I feel like a wedding car with a tin can still traveling behind it, years and years after the event. I mean, I haven't been obsessed to the point where it has destroyed my life. I have a lovely wife and a grown daughter who has been a great joy to me. We live in a pleasant condo in La Mesa, California, with a cat the color of cinnamon, named Joy-Hulga. I have season tickets at nearby Jack Murphy Stadium where I watch the San Diego Padres perform. I have never mentioned Cory to my wife. In fact, I have never mentioned Cory to anyone, ever.

I have not done very many things in my life of which I am genuinely ashamed. But in the week following my evening with Cory I did three reprehensible things that will trail after me like pale ghosts all my life.

The first was that I did not go back to see Cory as I had promised. I wanted to. I planned to. But each evening as I made ready to walk over to Railroad Avenue, my throat tightened until I could barely swallow. Even away from her I could not think of a single word I could say. The anticipation of the long, crushing silences I knew lay ahead was too much for me. One day became two, three, six.

The second thing was worse and occurred a week to the day after our meeting. At midmorning I had to run an errand for my mother. I caught the bus downtown. The bus was small, painted red and cream, and held only about twenty people. It looked like a loaf of bread with windows and wheels. When I got on there were only three other passengers and one of them was Cory. She was sitting in a window seat just in front of the rear door. I lowered my eyes, took a seat at the front of the bus with my back to her. I rode the bus twenty blocks past the downtown, nearly to the end of the line, staring straight ahead, unseeing, my neck stiff as a railroad tie. When I stood up to leave I noted with great relief that Cory was gone.

What held me back? When I saw Cory why couldn't I have marched down the aisle and sat beside her? Why couldn't I have asked where she was going and then said something like "I guess we're both pretty shy, but maybe if we spend a little time together we'll get over the worst of it. Let's just walk around downtown for a while and window-shop. Maybe we'll get to be friends." And I would have taken Cory's hand, and she would have nestled her head against my shoulder. But then I've had nearly thirty-five years to compose that speech.

My third act occurred later that same day and made the other two forgettable. Eddie came by Kaz's place and the three of us tinkered with the truck. A couple of other sometime-ballplayers were hanging around.

"I hear you're travelin' with Cory Mazeppa," Eddie said to me.

"Where would you hear that?" I said.

"Cookie Brost saw you the other night. Nothin' happens in Northside that somebody doesn't see."

"So what?"

"Cory's hot stuff. Did you score?"

"What business is that of yours?"

"She took Kaz in the garage, more than once," said Eddie, leering, his mouth twisted. "And me." He danced backward a few steps. "So, what about you?"

Everyone was waiting. They were all watching me.

"She was easy," I said.

Northside and the city of which it is a suburb are not places where people buy books. They are rough, ethnically mixed, hard-working communities, distinctly lacking in imagination. I insisted the city be on my itinerary when I ventured out to promote *Murder's Blue Gown*. My mother had visited California once or twice a year, spending the money from Nick Walczak's dairy herd on airfare and hotels. I had not been back to Northside since the time about a month after my evening with Cory, when my mother sprang the surprise that she was marrying Nick and we were moving to Wisconsin.

I arrived the night before Cory's funeral. Coincidence? I suppose. A bitter wind drifted snow over the city. I bought a newspaper, found the ad touting my appearance at a bookstore the following evening, and scanned the obituaries, where I saw: "MAZEPPA, Corrina Ann (Kliciak). Suddenly, on Feb. 22; she is survived by . . ."

The names of her four children, her parents, and her sisters followed. The oldest child was named James. Another coincidence, I suppose.

Nick Carraway in *The Great Gatsby* states, "Everyone suspects himself of at least one of the cardinal virtues." His, he says later, was honesty. I wonder about my own. It certainly isn't honesty. Is hindsight a virtue? Where do vice and virtue blur together? How responsible are we for the lives of those we touch briefly? Is omission as much of a sin as commission? I tried not to think about it. But I couldn't help it. I decided to attend the funeral of someone I hadn't seen for sixteen years, half my lifetime, half hers. Yet I felt strongly that I had contributed to her death. At that point I didn't know for certain how she died, but I would have bet my own life that she was a suicide.

I arranged for my mother to take a taxi down to the hotel and have dinner with me. For once I was vitally interested in her oral history of Northside. I had only to ask "What's new?" to elicit more information than I wanted to know about Cory and her family.

"Lots of excitement," my mother said, leaning conspiratorially across the dark blue linen tablecloth. "You remember Mazeppas, the family had the little store on Railroad Avenue, their second daughter, Cory, the one who married badly, committed suicide Monday. The old folks still live behind the store, though it's not a store anymore; they closed up after Safeway opened across Railroad Avenue in the big shopping center. Well, the suicide isn't official or anything. Mr. Mazeppa went to the bishop of their church; they have to have the funeral at a funeral home and not at the church, but she can be buried in their cemetery." And she went on and on and on.

"Hey, Flash." It was Eddie at my shoulder, just as he used to be near me at my locker in high school and at the continuous baseball game. I was crossing the parking lot toward the door of the funeral home. Eddie punched my shoulder, just as he did a half lifetime ago, with a backhanded flick of his knuckles.

"Eddie." I turned and smiled down at him, his thick glasses revealing the same blue blur as in the past. His hair was styled now, the ever present shoelace defeated. He wore an expensive black overcoat, a maroon velvet yarmulke perched on his skull like a beanie.

"Did you come all the way back here for the funeral?"

"Coincidence," I said, "though I might have, if I'd known in time."

We talked quietly about our present lives. We didn't mention Cory.

"How long since you've been home?" asked Eddie.

"Years," I said. *Home.* What a strange word. *Where the heart is* kept flashing through my head. *Where the heart is.* Not so untrue. This miserable, cold, inescapable city may well be where my heart is, I thought. A heart never grown to full size, suspended in the humid summer evenings of long ago: the baseball field, Cory, home.

"You'll see a lot of changes," Eddie said.

"I don't recognize much. The downtown has been leveled and rebuilt."

"So has the old neighborhood. The Railroad Hotel's still there, but there's an auto dealership between the hotel and Mazeppas' store. There's a K Mart where we used to play baseball. Store's a block square, dropped right down on the old playing field like a circus tent. You wouldn't know the place."

At this moment Kaz appeared, getting out of a bronze limousine longer than the funeral cars parked at the side of the building.

"This guy's a wheel," said Eddie, grinning, displaying Kaz to me like a personal accomplishment.

"I guess none of us have done so badly, us three old ballplayers," I said, shaking Kaz's hand. Kaz looked every inch a millionaire: his hands were as soft and pink as his face, which was turning fleshy. In a few years he would look like a friendly bulldog.

We sat shoulder to shoulder on one of the varnished pews of the funeral home. The service was brief, the chapel less than half full. The coffin was closed. A relief. I could never have brought myself to walk by it.

"Those were the best of times," said Eddie, smiling sadly. We were back in the parking lot waiting for Kaz's limousine. He had offered to drop Eddie at work, me at my hotel. "God, I remember springing out of bed in the morning, wolfing down whatever I could find for breakfast, grabbing my glove, and heading for the field. I was almost grown up before I realized how poor we were."

"I always knew how poor we were," said Kaz.

"But what was it about baseball?" I said. "Why did we spend three or four years of our lives on that playing field?"

"It was something to do with the ritual," said Eddie. "There was a wonderful sameness, a stability. At that age you don't understand anything that's happening to your body or your life. Kids at that age think they're immortal; they don't want their parents' religion, if the parents have any . . ."

"There was something primitive about the game," said Kaz. "A closeness to the earth. The hardest part was waiting for the field to dry out after the snow melted. We'd try but we'd never make it, would we?"

"We'd be playing with the water over our shoes. Remember how clots of mud used to cling to the ball."

"I can still see the spray flying when I hit it square on."

"Let's drive by the field," said Kaz. And he gave the driver instructions, not giving Eddie or me a chance to object.

"Baseball is healing," I said. "I wish I could put it better, but the feeling I had, though I didn't know it then, is like I feel after being with a woman who loves me a lot, that dreamy lethargy, that feeling of well-being."

People stared at us as we got out of the limousine in the K Mart parking lot. Kaz and Eddie looked like Mafia hitmen; I looked like a poor cousin in my light jacket and slippery shoes. The sky was low, the air bitter; snow drifted around our ankles. Across the street Mazeppas' store sat forlorn and in need of paint. There were curtains drawn across the front windows, and what used to be the door to the grocery was drifted full of snow and street refuse.

Inside K Mart it was bright as summer noon. The ceiling was paved with white lights. There were few shoppers in the store. A bedraggled mother pushed a silver cart with two children in it. Another was tugging at her coat, whining.

"The backstop and home plate would be over there," said Kaz, pointing to the women's wear section, where circular dollies full of bright, cheap clothes were crowded together like a field of giant flowers.

"Left field would be out there in the furniture department," said Eddie.

We walked to the sporting goods section. There was little baseball equipment on display. But Kaz and Eddie found gloves while I took the only bat in sight. Kaz spotted baseballs, safely behind glass in a display case. He looked around. As usual in K Mart, there were no salespeople anywhere in sight. Kaz went behind the counter, slid open the case, and extracted a half-dozen baseballs. Kaz and Eddie took off their overcoats and laid them across the counter. We made our way to women's wear. I took a child's red dress from a dolly and dropped it to mark the spot where home plate would be. Kaz paced off the distance to the pitcher's mound, elbowing dress racks out of the way, clearing a path. Eddie sprinted for the outfield. "Hit me a good one, Flash," he sang.

I held the bat high, gripped tight at the end. I held it straight up and down, peeking over the crook of my left elbow. I have always prided myself that I was using a stance and grip remarkably similar to Carl Yaztrezemski's, ten years before he first appeared in the majors. Kaz pawed the cheap white tiles where the mound used to be. Far back in left Eddie drifted among the sofas and loveseats.

"Burn it in there, Kaz," he hollered, shielding his eyes with his glove, blocking out the glare of an imaginary sun. A few people were staring at us, warily, as they passed in nearby aisles.

I wiggled the end of the bat and waited. As I did, the white light of K Mart became summer sunshine. The store lifted away from us like a bell jar. The other players took their places on the field: tall, silent Ted Troy at first base, Peppy Goselin as shortstop, Pudge Green in center field. As the players took shape, the racks of pink and blue dresses, the women's and children's clothes, fresh as sunshine, smelling of ironing and starch, rose like mist. The grass was emerald-green, measled with dandelions.

"Burn it in there, Kaz," shouted Eddie.

Kaz fired the ball. I swung and fouled it off. Strange that it made a sound like breaking glass. Someone strange was walking in from right field, a young man, his face the color of maple, wearing a white shirt buttoned to the collar and a black-on-white name tag reading AHMED. He looked both puzzled and frightened. "Please not to do what it is you are doing, please," he said in a heavy accent. He raised his hands in a gesture similar to calling time in baseball, though I'm sure he had no idea what he was doing.

Kaz snarled several words at the intruder. He scuttled away.

"Come on, Flash, straighten one out," yelled Eddie.

"I lied about Cory," I yelled.

"Everybody lies about things like that," said Kaz.

"You?"

"Everybody." He made a gesture that encompassed us all.

All the players were in place now, my team along the sidelines, Kaz's team in the field. All the baseball boys. All the accountants and thugs and TV producers and packing-plant workers and railroad section men. And Cory was sitting on the grass a few yards behind the bench, alone as always, her black hair snarled about her face, her mauve dress spread in a wide arc about her.

There were two pinging sounds like a doorbell. "Security to Section 12. Security to Section 12," said a female voice.

"Burn it in there, Kaz."

Cory is dead and her death stays with me, trapped here with me, inside my own skin.

The maple-faced boy was back and there was someone with him. Someone larger.

"Please not to do what it is you are doing, please."

"Fire the ball."

"Security to Section 12."

What were these strange people doing on the field? The earth felt hard, my feet refused to dig in properly.

"Pitch the ball."

Kaz wound up; his thick arm and ham-like hand with the grease-stained knuckles snapped the ball toward me.

Cory smiled shyly. After the game I'd walk her to the end of the sidewalk, kiss her so gently in the lilac shadows.

The ball was one long laser of white connecting Kaz's hand with my bat. In the hairsbreadth of a second between the crack of the bat and the ball exploding into the sun above the outfield, I relished the terrible joy of hitting it square on.

The
Valley of the Schmoon

IT'S NICE OF YOU to ride along with me, Artie. I'm glad you let me talk you into it. I usually travel alone — I mean, how many guys are there who are afraid to fly anymore? Everyone flies, and likes it. I fly, too. I do. Have to, to keep my job. But this time, what with three days from the end of spring training until we're due in Seattle . . . duck soup, an easy drive for an old roadrunner like me.

Yeah, I hafta fly on the long road trips. I mean, I can boogie down to Oakland from Seattle, jump in the car right after a game. It's about fifteen hours. Get in in time to catch forty winks and head for the ballpark. But the long hauls, like from Seattle to K.C., or the Eastern swing: New York, Boston, Toronto, no way. I get boiled as a boot, Artie. I'm stiff as a duffel bag full of bats by the time the skipper guides me to a seat. The old Foxx isn't a bad guy for a manager. Knows his baseball, treats his coaches like human beings. I'm goin' into my third year with the Mariners. There are places I'd rather be, but when you're old as me you take anything just to stay in the game.

You don't have to worry about that for a few years, eh, Artie? Second stop in the Bigs; Mariners gave up their best infielder to get you. Don't expect the team to have a winning season, but, God, you've got a batting eye, and you can hit the curve ball. You'll be in the Bigs for ten, fifteen years, easy. What did you play, ten, twelve games with Milwaukee? Okay, fourteen. You'll still qualify as a rookie this year. You'll win Rookie of the Year, no contest. Wait and see. You can trust the old coach. I know pure baseball talent when I see it.

Your folks probably took you on airplanes when you were a kid, right? I figured. My old man took all us kids on the subway to Coney Island once. That's all the travelin' I did until I got into minor-league baseball. Travel was all by bus down there. Hell, when I broke into the majors we still traveled by train, everybody did. Those were the days, Artie. Things were more relaxed. We played a lot of jokes. We were real practical jokers. Pretty silly stuff, Artie. Short-sheeting a guy's berth . . .

You know the story of what the old-timers did to the Babe when he broke in? He was a chucker then, you know.

Oh, sure. I forgot you been to college. Is that right? I didn't know he won that many games. Yeah, well, the good ol' boys told the Babe that all the pitchers slept with their arms in a sling at the side of their berth while they was travelin'. The Babe fell for it, and he was so stove up after sleepin' like that for a few nights that he had to miss a couple of turns in the rotation. They say the manager really gave the veterans shit for that trick, but that he was winkin' behind his hand the whole time.

Boy, look at that moon, Artie. Ain't she a beaut? It's like the mountains was silver, and if there wasn't a windshield there, we could reach right out and touch the stars.

I suppose you're too young to have ever seen me play. I played my last game in '52. Ended my career with the Cardinals.

Geez, is that right? You weren't born until '60? I got kids older'n you. I was screwin' before you were born. I always wanted a son I could say that to, when he got to be a mouthy teenager. Your father ever say that to you, Artie? Naw. He's a big wheel with Shell Oil, didn't you say? I guess executives don't say that kind of thing to their sons. Also, you probably weren't a mouthy teenager. You're not born-again, are you, Artie? Thank God. That was a joke, Artie. That's better.

Three daughters, that's what I had. One minute they were pretty little girls, and then I gave them away at their weddings. I think I missed a lot being on the road all my working life. Don't ever let baseball take over your life, Artie. You won't, I'm sure. You're gonna make more this year than I made in my whole career as a player. Ten years, and you can retire with dignity. Yeah, well, no use cryin' over spilled milk, as my old mother used to say, God rest her soul.

I don't know, somehow I always figured things was gonna turn out better. I wonder if everybody feels that way? I wonder if everybody feels as down as I do? Where'd you say you were from, Artie? Wamsutter, Wyoming. Do people get depressed in Wamsutter? All that mountain air and big sky . . . yeah, well, I guess a trailer out in the desert ain't exactly Fifth Avenue. Oh, I see, you lived in Salt Lake since you were fourteen.

Somehow I just figured there was more to life. Not that things haven't been okay, Artie, you know what I mean? How many guys get to manage a big-league team? Three of them, even if I never lasted a whole season anywhere. And coach. I mean, I'm only the catcher's coach now. They just invented that position in the last few seasons. But I'm still in baseball and that means a lot to me.

When I played, there was a manager, third- and first-base coaches, and maybe a pitching coach. First base was usually a burnout, an old plug who'd put in his years and couldn't do nothin' outside of baseball. A likeable guy who'd taken one too many high, hard ones without a batting helmet . . . sissy goddamned things, them and seat belts, and batting gloves, sliding gloves, and wristbands. All the guts are gone out of baseball, Artie. We maybe weren't as fast as you guys today, but we were a tough bunch of mothers. A carload of cry babies now. Whinin' if they don't get to fly first class.

You probably been told already, but some of the players think of me as a burned-out case. I know what gets said behind my back. Maybe it's true. I'll be sixty-five in a year, then they'll probably give me the old pink slip. I wonder what the hell I'll do? I'll probably just up and die. I'd like to be buried in an outfield in a park that's still got grass, and not that goddamned double-knit turf.

In the old days there was none of this keepin' fit all winter long. Hell, Artie, you come to spring training in better shape than we used to be in in August. We'd slouch into camp in the spring, twenty, thirty, or forty pounds overweight. We never did anything more strenuous in the off-season than bend our elbows and push ourselves back from the table after a big meal. Me and Lefty Lupul, you must remember him — won twenty games for the Cards in '44 — used to do nothin' but hunt. We'd sit out in the duck blind with some thick sandwiches and our buddy Jack Daniels. Those were the days, Artie. Gone forever, though . . .

The Baseball Encyclopedia has my nickname listed as "Comic Book." Can you believe that? I mean, I read 'em. What's wrong with that? Never see a comic book in the locker room anymore. A few fuck books. You figure in some future edition of *The Baseball Encyclopedia* a player will be nicknamed "Fuck Book" Slagle? That was a joke, Artie.

Where have all the nicknames gone from baseball, Artie? Just look around the league. Have you ever seen such a collection of Bobs, Daves, Georges, Brians, and . . . Arties. In the old days we had Harry the Cat, and Harry the Hat, Joltin' Joe, and the Brat. There's been Shoeless Joe, and Gettysburg Eddie Plank, the Iron Man, Suitcase Simpson, Redleg Snyder, Germany Schaefer, and Bucketfoot Al Simmons. What's your nickname, Artie? I figured. Hey, did you ever hear of an old-timer, name of Bob Ferguson? You know what his nickname was? Death to Flying Things. Can you believe that? I wonder how he got a name like that? Look around you today: Tony (no nickname) Gwynn just won a batting title, and the big stars are Steve Garvey, Pete Rose, Jack Morris, Fernando Valenzuela. Not a nickname among them.

Take Dave Winfield. Winfield killed a sea gull one night a couple of years ago. Press made a big fuss. Dipsticks in Toronto arrested him, charged him with cruelty to animals, then let him go. But is *he* called Death to Flying Things? No. Nicknames are dead, Artie. Guys like you who make half a million a year and are gonna make a million want to be addressed as Mister, not as Nosey, or Pinky, or Preacher, or Death to Flying Things. No offense, Artie, that's just the way of the world. But I'm gettin' more and more out of touch with the world every year.

Yes, sir, "Comic Book Demarco" is how I'm listed. You know what my favorite was? *Li'l Abner*. Geez but I cried when Al Capp stopped drawin' that strip. Are you old enough to have ever read it? You seen the movie on TV. That's life. Everything a short cut. How long were you in the minors, Artie? One year. Geez, one year. I was six years in Triple A in Montreal. I practically learned how to speak French I was there so long. Then I was only in the Bigs for four years, never played full-time; I was all washed up at thirty. You know what I hit? My lifetime average was .312. You can look it up. How many catchers today can hit .312? I was twenty-five years ahead of my time. Son of a bitch. Most I ever made as a player was fifteen thousand dollars. You young guys tip more than that in a year.

There were real comic strips in the old days, Artie: *Li'l Abner, Joe Palooka, Pogo, Little Orphan Annie*. Where have all the good comics gone? I can't understand a word of *Doonesbury* . . . a bunch of ex-hippie war protesters as far as I can make out. And *Bloom County*, I don't know what that guy's talkin' about. Even *Garfield*. You know, when that one started out, Garfield was a real cat, a fat, scruffy tomcat with no respect for nobody. And what did they do to him? They made him *cute*. Gave him big eyes and orange fur, and now every window's got a Garfield toy in it. Only that old busybody *Mary Worth* is left. But I never read her. Geez, Artie, even the comics have passed me by.

Al Capp. Now there was a real cartoonist. His name was Alfred Caplin, a tough dude, patriotic as John Wayne, had an artificial leg. I think maybe he lost it in the war.

You watch the soap operas, Artie? That's good. Don't ever start. Most of today's players watch them. One son of a bitch on our own team, who I won't name, got it in his contract that he can watch an afternoon soap. Can you imagine even suggestin' to Horace Stoneham, Walter O'Malley, or Gussie Busch that you wanted to watch a soap opera? National League team we got this guy from was forced to trade him, either that or keep him on the bench every time they played at Wrigley.

You know what happened to Al Capp? Died of a broken heart. Died of embarrassment, the poor son of a bitch. Ham Fisher, the guy who drew *Joe Palooka*, offed himself. Walt Kelly up and died, too. *Barney Google* and *Snuffy Smith*, *The Gumps*, *Tillie the Toiler*, all the good comics, all the good artists, gone.

Hey, sorry there, Artie. I didn't mean to break down like that. It's all right for a man to cry. I seen it on *Donahue*. Sure I can drive. I'll be okay. Just let me blow my honker here, clear my head and all. Really, it's okay. I could drive these mountains blindfolded.

You ever hear the story of what happened to Al Capp? It was the pinkos got him, you know. Back when all that Vietnam shit was goin' on, when everybody was disrespectin' the flag, burnin' buildings on campuses and pourin' blood on the Pentagon and stuff like that, why Al Capp was offended just like any good American. Through his comic strip he took on those war protesters, especially that Joan Baez woman. He drew some strips about a character called Joannie Phony, that fit that folk singer to a tee. He took on all them traitors and cowards, and he did America proud.

But in the end they got him. Lust. If you don't already know, Artie, a stiff cock knows no politics. Bunch of those protester types, they set him up. Some young chickie went up to his office and told him how she admired him and how, wouldn't it be nice if they should have sex. And, I mean, Artie, who could refuse an offer like that? Everybody's human, right? But there was a terrible law in that state, and them protesters used it, charged poor Al Capp with something like Having Sex with Somebody Other than Your Wife, or some such dumb charge. They had him dead to rights. He pleaded no contest. I don't think there was even a fine. But the embarrassment. It wasn't long until he retired. Stopped the strip. Then, before you know it, he was dead. Sad, Artie, sad.

No, really, I'm okay. Naw, naw, I don't need to stop. We'll stop for coffee in a couple of hours, soon as we get over the mountains. Usually when I get to feelin' depressed I have a cigar, but you notice how considerate I been, haven't had a cigar in the car on the whole trip. I appreciate you bein' clean livin', Artie. Geez, that brings something else to mind: in the old days we were pretty bad bastards, used to hoist a few whenever the occasion called for it. We'd get rowdy sometimes, too. Year I was with the Pirates, manager had to bail a bunch of us out of the slammer more than once. But these guys now, not rowdy, just spacemen, dancin' in slow motion in the on-deck circle. I mean a guy takes a foul on the shin and walks it off for about five minutes, 'cause to him only a few seconds have passed. I hate to see that, Artie. Drugs are something else I don't understand.

Being all alone in the world is tough, too, Artie. My old lady, she was something else. Right from the old neighborhood. Lucy Allesandrini: hair down to her shoulders, brown eyes you could drown in. She was a virgin when I married her.

She was, is, a good woman. But things change. Nothin' ever stays the same, and nothin's ever as good as you figure it's gonna be. After the youngest daughter got married, Lucy, she moved out, too. She's done okay for herself; she's married to a guy owns six Ace Hardware stores, comes home every night regular as clockwork. "We're gonna have a nice old age together," she said to me. No hard feelings. She didn't even ask for bread or property or nothin'. I'da felt better if she had.

Oh, sorry, I just can't keep very good control of myself tonight.

Let me tell you another story about Al Capp and *L'il Abner*. You ever hear of the Valley of the Schmoon? No, shit, they don't ski there! Okay, I knew you were joking.

I bet you don't even know what a schmoo is. There weren't any schmoos in the movie, at least not that I can remember. Schmoos were little pear-shaped creatures that looked like bowling pins with arms and legs, human features, and cat's whiskers. They were totally obliging. They gave milk and laid eggs. If you were hungry they'd leap willingly into the frying pan. If your mouth was waterin' for chicken-fried steak, that's what they'd taste like. If you were cold they made you warm. In other words they supplied all the creature comforts. And they were happy makin' people happy. All the schmoos lived in the Valley of the Schmoon, an absolutely perfect place. And every once in a while some would spill over into the real world. But the government knew they had to be destroyed. Because if people had schmoos they'd never be hungry, thirsty, unhappy, tired, or cold. No one would go to work. The world would stop functioning. The government understood that society could only operate when individuals have to strive for necessities. So they'd send out the troops and kill the schmoos, and drive those that survived back to the Valley of the Schmoon.

You know, Artie, I spend a lot of my time dreamin' on these long cross-country drives and all winter in that empty house in New Jersey. I dream about things bein' perfect, about finding the Valley of the Schmoon.

I haven't told you this before, have I? If I start to repeat myself you just leap in. I get a little confused sometimes. I forget who I told which stories to. Too many foul tips off the old noggin. I got hit with a bat once. Did I tell you that one? Ted Williams did it. In an exhibition game during spring training; I was way up on my toes, and just toppled forward as he swung, and *wham!* He hit the top of the mask, knocked it foul past third base, took a chip outa my ear here, see. It's okay. I can keep the car on the road and still show you my ear. I was in the hospital for two weeks. Doc said a quarter of an inch more, and it would have been morgue city for me.

I don't think I ever been the same since I took that wallop on the old bean. I was *inside* a couple of times, you know. Same state hospital where they stored Jimmy Piersall in a foam-rubber room. I was supposed to see a shrink twice a week after they let me out the last time. But that was six, seven years ago — I never went. I mean, all I did was cut the *backs* of my wrists. That is kinda laughable, ain't it, Artie? Pull up my shirt sleeve there and you can see the scar. Well, okay, you seen one scar you seen 'em all. Soon as we get through the mountains we'll stop for coffee.

When I really get depressed I think more and more about the Valley of the Schmoon. You know, a place where everything is perfect. I figure if there was such a place it might be down in one of these valleys here in these mountains. I figure I might be able to find it on a night like this when the moon turns everything silver, and the evergreen trees look like they're covered in tinsel. You know what I'm gonna do? I got it all figured out, Artie. One of these overpasses on the interstate — gonna hit it at about ninety miles per hour. Hey, don't look at me like that. Not this trip. You're in good hands.

I'll be alone when I do it. No alcohol. No suicide note. I wouldn't do that to my kids. I'll just stop, take a tire wrench, and loosen the bolts on one front wheel. Then, *wham,* right into the overpass. It'll be an accident. Another old ballplayer gone. "Poor old coach just fell asleep at the wheel," is what they'll say.

If you ever read about that happenin', Artie, you could maybe suggest another nickname for me. I could be known as Overpass Demarco. It'd make a good trivia question. Strikes me that there's somethin' sad about Comic Book as a nickname for a man goin' on sixty-five; though Lucy and most of my friends call me Bookie.

There was a lot of what you'd call camaraderie in the old days. Guys hung around together even in the off-season. The word *club* had real meaning in those days. You had to earn your way inside. Hazing. Hey, there was a lot of that went on. I guess that's gone the way of nicknames, eh? Anybody do anything to you when you came up with Milwaukee? Yeah, they took you out to dinner. And they won't do nothin' here either. Management's afraid you might sprain a finger. Let me tell you a story or two. If we took a rookie out to dinner he'd find a mouse in his mousse, you know what I mean? One of the guys I played with carried a little twist of amber cellophane, and he'd have the bartender plant it in a rookie's drink. He'd be right beside the rookie when he drained his glass and found the cellophane. "What the hell's that?" the kid would say. And my friend would say, "Guess you never noticed when I spit in your drink," and he'd flash a smile with his mouth all full of tobacco. I've seen kids puke right on the floor, Artie. God, but we used to laugh our guts out. And we'd fix every rookie up with this chick that was really a guy. We'd tell the rookie how the chick liked to be felt up. We'd plant them in a nice cozy booth in the corner, then we'd all be peerin' over the divider to watch the kid's expression when he got to the chick's balls. Things were a lot simpler in the old days, Artie. Yeah, right. Hazing would have to be a lot more sophisticated in this day and age. I mean, you got an agent. You don't haze a guy who's got an agent. We used to live day to day. Hand to mouth. You got a contract good for five years even if your rotator cuff cracks like a windowpane the first day of the season. Am I right? Yer darn tootin'. That's what an agent can do for you.

We didn't have enough money to head for the Bahamas or some-place exotic the second the season was over. All you guys have corporate offices in Dallas, or Miami, and you head for your Mr. Bigstar Enterprises to set up some new bank loans, buy a copper mine, or a high-rise, as a tax write-off. Got you there, eh? I knew you already bought an apartment. How many stories? Twelve. Hit thirty home runs this season and you can buy a thirty-story building to celebrate.

By the time they retire me, and I ain't gonna go until they shove me out the door, I'll have the old house in Jersey paid off. Figured Lucy and I would retire there. I get real sad when I think about Lucy. Did I tell you all this before, Artie? I forget what I been talkin' about sometimes. It was a nice house when we bought it in '49. But the neighborhood's changed. The block's full of foreign people with hot cars and loud radios, and they own dogs . . .

I hope you have a happier marriage than me, Artie. You're engaged, right? I never seen her, but I can guess, nice girl from Salt Lake named Heather or Cheryl? Margaret. Yeah, right. I bet she *is* an old-fashioned girl. You don't call her Maggie or Muggsy, I bet. Hey, I'm not puttin' you down. Don't get me wrong. Just the changing times. You know even the Baseball Sadies ain't as tough as they used to be. Rough and ready broads. But goodhearted, most of them. One gal, name of Big Mona, in Pittsburgh I think it was; she must of had slow-actin' clap. Infected the whole goddamned team, except the shortstop and second baseman, who were gay, except in those days we didn't say gay. That wasn't too long after they invented penicillin, and the old team sawbones sure had fun drivin' a needle big as a railroad spike into the ass of every player on the team, yours truly included. We brought in Big Mona and got her fixed up, too. There was no hard feelings. Just a lot of kidding and horsing around. I wonder whatever happens to Baseball Sadies? I wonder where Big Mona is tonight? If she ain't cashed in, she's close to my age. Over the hill and down the mountain.

I bet your lady went to a girls' school. Does she wear a green blazer and leg warmers? You're not gonna drag her along after you get married, are you? Women on the road are a disruptive force. She's a what? A fucking psychologist! Great. When you go into a slump she can analyze you until you come out of it. When I'd be 0–30, my old lady used to say, "Think of the kids, Bookie. How are we gonna feed 'em if you lose your job?" I'd just think about bein' a box boy for my fat-assed brother-in-law who owns a supermarket in Camden. That would squeeze a hit or two out of me.

Did I tell you I used to hunt with Snuffy Stirnweiss? You must have heard of Snuffy. Great infielder with the Yankees. We used to go up to Ontario and hunt ducks every fall. Poor Snuffy, he bought it on the Amtrak on the way to New York one day. Some switch went wrong and a couple of cars telescoped. God, Artie, it's been over twenty-five years since Snuffy cashed in.

Life is depressing, Artie. Don't ever forget that.

Geez, feel that pull on the wheel, Artie. I gotta park for a minute. I got good tools; I'll fix it in no time. Look at that silver valley below us. The Valley of the Schmoon, Artie; it's right down there.

Okay, I'll just ease her over to the side. Hate to stop on a downgrade like this. Look at that overpass down there, Artie. Moonlight makes it bright as day out here. Look at the color they paint those things these days. Bright orange . . .

Hey, where are you goin'? You don't want to get out here. At least wait until I get the car completely stopped. There ain't a town either way for thirty-five . . . miles . . . .

Geez, was it somethin' I said?

Look at that son of a bitch run. If they can teach him how to bunt he'll beat out an infield hit or two.

Well, with him out of the car I can at least have a cigar. Rookies. They never learn. Hell, I'd been in the majors for three years before I ever heard the word *sophisticated*. Let's see, by the time I get to Seattle it will be four A.M. That'll be seven in the East. I can phone Lucy before she goes to work . . . .

Punchlines

PASCOE AND MARTINEZ came to visit me at Vancouver General Hospital the day after I picked up forty-one stitches from running through the glass wall next to the front door of my girlfriend's apartment building.

Pascoe is black, but beside Martinez he looks gray. Martinez is new to the team; his home is in the Dominican Republic; he comes from that famous town where they have a factory that turns out iron-armed shortstops who gobble up ground balls like they were *Pac-Man*. Martinez speaks only about ten words of English, so he's happy to have anybody pay any attention to him. He has worried brown eyes and is so black his round cheeks and wide forehead give off a glare in bright sunlight. Martinez doesn't know he's getting himself in the manager's bad books, making himself an outcast by hanging around with me. Pascoe does.

My name is Barry McMartin. Reporters describe me as the Vancouver Canadians' designated flake. The team bad boy. A troublemaker. Most of my teammates don't like me very much, in fact most are a little afraid of me. Some of them think I'm on drugs. There's more than the usual hassle about athletes and drugs in these post-Len Bias days. But I've never done drugs. I have some common sense, even if most people tend to think the amount I have is minimal.

At the hospital, Pascoe stuck his head around the doorjamb and when he saw me he said, "How the hell did you get all the way to Triple A on one fucking brain cell?"

I smiled, though it hurt like hell. Nine of those stitches were in my hairline. Martinez grinned his greeting, showing off his white eyes and teeth. He said something in Spanish, ending by clapping his hands once and doing a little dance step. I assume he was wishing me well.

"How long will you be out of action this time?" Pascoe asked. He is our first baseman. This is his third year in Triple A, and he's not likely to go any higher. He is six foot seven and shaves his head to resemble Otis Sistrunk, the football player; he looks mean as a boil, but one of the reasons he's never had a shot at the Bigs is that he lacks the killer instinct. He plays an average first base, but for such a big man he has only warning-track power as a hitter.

"Management put me on the fifteen-day disabled list. I'll be ready to go in less than that. The doctors said I was real lucky. 'You are very lucky you're not dead,' is what the doctor in emergency said to me as he was sewing up my cuts. 'A couple of guys get killed every month by doing what you did tonight. You must have a guardian angel; it's a miracle you didn't permanently disable yourself. You'll be back playing baseball inside of two weeks.' "

I pulled up my hospital gown and showed the guys the rest of my stitches. The cuts made a primitive mark of Zorro on my chest. None were deep, not even close to a tendon or a vital artery. What did scare me almost to death at the time was that a shard of glass clipped off the tip of my right earlobe and I bled like a stuck pig. When I recovered my senses, I was lying in a pool of blood and broken glass in the entranceway to Judy's apartment building. I thought I was a goner for sure.

"Well, what are we gonna do to cheer our friend up, Marty?" Pascoe says, with a smile that goes halfway to his ears.

"Sí," says Martinez.

"Tell me a joke," I say.

"We know he can't play baseball, lady. We want to use him for second base," says Pascoe, and we both break up, while Martinez watches us, mystified. My laughter lasts only a few seconds before pain from my stitches brings me up short.

One night last season, soon after I became Pascoe's roommate, we stayed up all night telling jokes. We were sitting in a twenty-four-hour café called the Knight & Day, and we just kept drinking coffee and telling stories until the sun came up. We both agreed that we'd told every joke, clean or dirty, that we both knew. And as we got to know each other better we decided that instead of retelling a whole story we'd just shout out the punchline. We both knew the joke so we could both laugh. To give an example, there's a long shaggy-dog story about a white man trying to prove himself to the Indian tribe he's living with. The Indians give him a list of acts to perform that will establish his courage. When he comes back to camp looking happy but torn to rat shit, one of the Indians says to him, "You were supposed to *kill* the bear and *make love* to the woman." So now instead of retelling that story we just shout out the punchline and both of us, and anyone else who knows the story, have a good laugh. But it stymies some of the other players and doesn't go over well when we're out on dates.

"The trouble was the pilot was gay," I say, and this time Martinez laughs along.

Martinez is so congenial we are genuinely trying to teach him English. Not like some of the Spanish-speaking players. We've been known to take them to restaurants and have them say to the waitress, thinking that they're ordering a hamburger, "I'd like to eat your pussy, please."

"What did management have to say?" Pascoe asks, changing the subject. There is genuine concern on his face.

"When you get to my balls try to act as if nothing unusual is happening," I reply. That's a punchline from a joke about Sonny Crocker going undercover, dressed as a woman. "Hey, the nurses

here are terrific, there was this one last night pulled the screen close
around my bed . . ."

"I'm serious," says Pascoe.

"So am I."

"Goddamnit, Barr. How much trouble are you in?"

"Well, Skip didn't come down. As you know, Skip hates my guts.
Skip wanted to fire my ass. Or so says Osterman. But I'm too
valuable for them to do that. Milwaukee's going to call me up inside
of a month — see if they don't. So it was Old Springs came down
himself."

Springs is what we call Osterman, the general manager of the
baseball team. He is one of these dynamic guys who walks like he's
got springs in his shoes, and he's read all these inspirational books
like *How to Fuck Your Friends, Rip Off Your Neighbors, and Make
a Million by Age 30.* He's always talking to us ballplayers about long-
term investments, five-year plans, and networking.

"You're an asshole, McMartin," he said to me. "You're a fuck-up,
you're an asshole, you're a jerk. You're also a criminal. If it wasn't
for baseball, your ass would be in jail in some town out in the
Oklahoma desert, or you'd be in a psych hospital, which is where *I*
think you belong. Skip said he'd personally kill you if he visited you
himself. So he sent me. For some reason he figures I have more self-
control. Skip says to tell you he wishes you'd cut your troublemaking
throat when you fell through that window, or whatever you did."

"Yeah, well, you tell Skip his wife's not bad in bed. But she's not
nearly as good as your wife."

I was sorry as soon as the words were out. I knew I'd gone too far,
again. I don't really want these guys to hate me. I just want to make
it clear that I don't take shit from *anybody.*

"You really are pure filth, McMartin," Springs growls. "The front
office personnel voted unanimously not to send you flowers or wish
you a speedy recovery. Unfortunately, in Milwaukee they don't
know what an asshole you are; they think you might be able to hit
thirty home runs for them next year. They'd let fucking Charles
Manson bat cleanup if they thought he'd hit thirty homers. But just
let me remind you, the minimum wage in Oklahoma is about three-

fifty an hour, and out of a baseball uniform you're not even worth that."

"Try to imagine how little I care," I said.

"We're going to tell the press you were being chased out of the apartment by an angry husband," said Springs. "It will fit your image and make you look less like a fool. But let me tell you, Milwaukee is fed up with your antics, too. This is absolutely the last time."

"Did management suspend you, or what?" asks Pascoe.

"Naw, I told you, I'm their fair-haired boy. I'm on the D.L. for fifteen days. I'll be out of this hospital tomorrow morning. So while you guys fuck off to Portland and Phoenix and get your asses whipped eight out of nine without your favorite cleanup hitter, I'll be sitting in Champagne Charlie's pounding a Bud and drooling over the strippers."

"I should have that kind of luck," says Pascoe. "I don't know, Barry, you got to stop acting so . . . so external, man," he added, shaking his head sadly.

I should treat Pascoe better. He's a decent guy. I don't know why he hangs around with me. Lately everything I touch seems to turn to shit. Pascoe's really a good friend. When I first arrived he showed me around Vancouver, which bars and clubs to visit, which to stay away from.

"Stay away from the King's Castle," he said to me as we walked down Granville Street one evening, heading toward Champagne Charlie's strip joint. "It's the biggest gay bar in Vancouver. Stay away from the Royal Bar, too. Bikers and Indians; half the people in the bar have shivs in their boots — and those are the women." There were flamingo neon bars above the entrance to the King's Castle and a dozen young men were standing in groups or lounging individually against the walls near the entrance, all caught in the pinkish glow of the neon.

"Fucking queers," I said as we passed, not caring if I was heard.

"Behave yourself," said Pascoe.

*

The first real *incident* happened the second week of the season. I have to admit I am naturally a loud person. I tend to shout when I speak; I walk with a bit of a swagger; I keep my head up and my eyes open. I've never minded being stared at. I like it that girls often turn and stare after me on the street.

The incident: there is a play in baseball called a suicide squeeze. A manager will call for it with a runner on third, and none or one out. As the pitcher goes into the stretch, the runner breaks from third; it is the hitter's duty to get the ball on the ground anywhere in the ballpark, though they usually try to bunt it between the pitcher and third or first. The idea is that by the time the ball is fielded, the base runner will have scored, the fielder's only play being to first. If, however, the hitter misses the pitch, the base runner is dead, hence the term suicide squeeze.

We were playing Phoenix in Vancouver, at Nat Bailey Stadium, a ballpark that, like the City of Vancouver, is clean and green; the only stadium in the Pacific Coast League that can compare to it is the one at the University of Hawaii, where the Islanders play part of their schedule. I tripled to lead off the second inning. Pascoe was batting fifth and he popped up weakly to the shortstop. The manager put on the suicide squeeze. The pitcher checked me, stretched, and delivered. I broke. The batter, a substitute fielder named Denny something, bunted, but he hit the ball way too hard. It was *whap! snap!* and the ball was in the pitcher's glove. He fired to the catcher, who was blocking the plate, and I was dead by fifteen feet. But I'd gotten up a real head of steam. I weigh 217 and stand six foot two, and I played a lot of football in high school back in Oklahoma. I hit the guy with a cross block that could have gotten me a job in the NFL. He was a skinny little weasel who looked like he was raised somewhere where kids don't get fed very often. I knocked him about five feet in the air, and he landed like he'd been shot in flight. The son of a bitch held on to the ball, though. The guy who bunted was at second before someone remembered to call time. They pried the ball out of the catcher's fingers and loaded him on a stretcher.

I'd knocked him toward our dugout and had to almost step over him to get to the bench. What I saw scared me. His neck was twisted at an awkward angle and he was bleeding from the mouth.

The umpire threw me out of the game for unsportsmanlike conduct. The league president viewed the films and suspended me for five games. The catcher had a concussion, a dislocated shoulder, and three cracked ribs. He's still on the D.L. as far as I know.

The next time I played against Phoenix, I got hit by a pitch the first time up. I charged the mound, the benches cleared, but before I even got to the pitcher, Pascoe landed on my back and took me right out of the play. Suddenly, there were three or four guys wrestling on top of us.

"Behave yourself," Pascoe hissed into my ear, as he held me pinioned to the ground, while players milled around us. Those have become Pascoe's favorite words as the summer has deepened, and I keep finding new ways to get into trouble.

Pascoe was happy when I started dating Judy. Word even got back to Skip, and he said a couple of civil words to me for the first time since I coldcocked the Phoenix catcher. Judy was a friend of a girl Pascoe dated a couple of times. She was a tiny brunette, a year younger than me, with dancing brown eyes, a student at the University of British Columbia, studying sociology.

"You're just shy," she said to me on our second date.

"Ha!" cried Pascoe. He and his girlfriend were sitting across from us in a Denny's.

"It's true," said Judy. "People who talk and laugh loudly in order to have attention directed to them are really very shy."

"You are, aren't you? Shy, I mean," Judy said later that evening in bed at her apartment. Our lovemaking had been all right, but nothing spectacular.

"I suppose," I said. "But I'd never admit it."

"You just did," said Judy, leaning over to kiss me.

The next thing that got me in bad with management was far worse than just coldcocking a catcher with a football block. Pascoe, Martinez, and I had been out making the rounds after a Saturday night game. I had several beers, but not enough that I should have been out of control. We closed up Champagne Charlie's, decided to walk home instead of taking a taxi. When we crossed the Granville Street bridge, the pre-dawn air was sweet and foggy. We were near Broadway and Granville, swinging along arm in arm, when the police cruiser pulled up alongside us.

The passenger window of the police car rolled down and an officer no older than Pascoe or me said, "Excuse me, gentlemen, but I'd like to see some identification."

Pascoe was reaching for his wallet when I said, "What the fuck are you hassling us for? We're minding our own business."

The officer ignored me, but he opened the door and stepped out, accepting the piece of ID Pascoe handed him.

Martinez, coming from a country where the police do not always exhibit self-control, stayed behind us, looking worried.

The officer returned Pascoe's ID. "And you, sir?" he said to Martinez.

"Leave him alone," I said. "He doesn't speak English."

"I'm not addressing you," the officer said to me.

"Fuck off," I yelled. "Leave him alone." I stepped in front of Martinez.

"Behave yourself," said Pascoe, and grabbed my arm. But I shoved him away, and before he could recover his balance, I shoved the officer back against the car. As the driver was getting out I leapt on the hood of the police car.

What happened next is a blur. I remember screaming curses at the police, dancing madly on the hood of the police car, feeling the hood dimple under my weight, dodging the grasping hands of the police and Pascoe.

I remember hearing Pascoe's voice crying out, "Oh, man, he's just crazy, don't shoot him." Then there was a hand on my ankle and I toppled sideways to the pavement. My mouth was full of blood and someone was sitting on me and my arms were being pulled behind my back and the handcuffs fastened.

I missed the Sunday afternoon game because management let me sit in jail until my court appearance Monday morning. The police had charged Martinez with creating a disturbance, but when a translator explained what had happened the prosecutor dropped the charge. I faced a half-dozen charges, beginning with assaulting a police officer.

The judge looked down at me where I stood, unshaven, my shirt torn and bloodstained, the left side of my face scraped raw from where I landed on the pavement. He remanded me for fourteen days for psychiatric evaluation.

"I'm not fucking crazy," I said to no one in particular.

The Vancouver Canadians' lawyer got on the phone to Milwaukee, and the Milwaukee Brewers' high-powered lawyers got in on the act. Before the end of the day, they struck a deal. If I agreed to spend an hour every afternoon with a private psychiatrist, the team would guarantee my good behavior, and my sentencing would be put off until the end of the baseball season.

Management had me by the balls. "You fuck up again and you're gone, kid," Skip said to me. "It doesn't matter how talented you are, you're not worth the aggravation."

I saw the shrink every afternoon for the whole home stand, weekends included. I took all these weird tests. Questions like "Are you a messenger of God?" and "Has your pet died recently?" I wore a jacket and tie to every session and talked a lot about what a nice girlfriend I had and how much I respected my parents.

"Well, Barry," the doctor said to me after about ten sessions, "you don't appear to have any serious problems, but I do wish you'd make an effort to be more cooperative. I am here to help you, after all."

"I thought I was being cooperative," I said innocently.

"In one sense you have been, but only partially. I find that you are mildly depressive, that you're anxious, under a lot of stress. Stress is natural in your profession, but I sense that there is something else bothering you, and I wish you'd level with me. To use an analogy, it is said that with a psychiatrist one tends to bare the body, scars and all, tear open the chest so to speak, and expose your innermost feelings. However, to date, you have scarcely taken off your overcoat."

"Look, I'm okay, honest. I had too much to drink, I got out of control. It won't happen again."

"Suit yourself," said the doctor.

My life leveled out for almost a month. We went on a road trip. I continued to hit well; I watched the American League standings, studied Milwaukee's box score in each day's newspaper, watched them fade out of the pennant race. I wondered how much longer it would be before I got my call to the Bigs. Once in Tacoma, Pascoe had to keep me from punching the lights out of a taxi driver who said something insulting about ballplayers, but other than that incident I stayed cool. I phoned Judy almost every night. I found myself doing with her what Pascoe so often did with me; I analyzed the game, dissected my at-bats pitch by pitch. I knew what I was saying wasn't very interesting for her, but it was a release for me, and not only did Judy not seem to mind, she gave the impression she enjoyed it.

I can't understand why I continue to fuck up. Judy brought two friends to a Sunday afternoon game. It was a perfect blue day and the stands at Nat Bailey Stadium are close enough to the field that I could look over at Judy and smile while I stood in the on-deck circle swinging a weighted bat. Her friends were a couple, Christine, a bouncy blonde with ringlets and a sexy way of licking her lips, and her husband, a wimpy guy who wore a jacket and tie and looked like he was shorter than Christine.

Although I had three hits and two RBIs, I wasn't in a good mood after the game. We went to one of these California-style restaurants with white walls and pink tablecloths, where everything is served in a sauce, and they look at you like you just shit on the floor if you ask for French fries. To top it off, I didn't like Trevor, and he didn't like me. I pounded about three Bud and then I drank a whole pitcher of this wine-cooler slop that tastes like Kool-Aid.

What really threw the shit into the fan was when the three of them decided the four of us would go to a movie, something called *Kiss of the Spider Woman*, about a couple of queers locked up in a prison in Argentina or someplace. Trevor gave us a little lecture about the *eloquent statement* the director was trying to make.

"There's no fucking way I'm going to a movie like that," I said, standing up to make my point.

"Barry, don't you dare make a scene," said Judy.

"No need to be boisterous about it," said Trevor. "You've simply been outvoted. We'd be happy to let you choose, but I don't think *The Texas Chainsaw Massacre* is showing in Vancouver at the moment."

I didn't say anything. I just grabbed the tablecloth and pushed everything across the table into Trevor's lap, then turned and stomped out.

I was surprised when Judy caught up with me a half block down the street.

"You were only half to blame for that scene," she said. "I'm always willing to go halfway," she added, taking my arm.

"I'd rather you went all the way," I said.

But things didn't go well back at her apartment.

"For goodness' sake, Barry, relax," Judy said. "You're still mad. Nobody can make love when they're mad."

But I was thrashing about the room; I'd pulled on most of my clothes by the time I got to the door. Ignoring the elevator, I ran down the stairs, realizing about halfway that I'd abandoned my shoes in Judy's apartment.

I crossed the lobby running full out, and it felt to me as if I was on one prolonged suicide squeeze, the catcher twenty feet tall, made of bricks, waiting with the ball, grinning. I didn't even slow down as I hit the wall of glass next to the door.

In spite of my bragging about spending my time in the strip joints while the team was on its road trip, I actually stayed out of downtown the whole time. Last night I met this chick at a club over on Broadway, near the University of British Columbia. She was with a date, but she knew who I was and made it pretty plain she liked me.

I made a late date for after the game tonight. I'm supposed to meet her at some white wine and fern restaurant in the financial district downtown, in the same building as the American embassy. Vicki is her name. She's tall with red-gold hair and freckles on her shoulders. Last night she was wearing a white sundress that showed off her tan.

"Bazoos that never quit," I said to Pascoe. "You should see her, man." I made a lapping motion with my tongue.

The game ended early. I took right up where I left off before the accident; I hit two dingers, a single, and stole a base. After each home run, I toured the bases slowly, my head erect, trying to look as arrogant as possible; I have a lot to prove to Skip, to management, to the self-righteous bastards I play with.

Sometimes I can't help but think about a note that was shoved through one of the vent slats in my locker at Nat Bailey Stadium. It was written on a paper towel from the washroom, printed in a childish scrawl. "Management pays Pascoe 300 a month to be you're freind," it said. For an instant my stomach dipped and I thought I might vomit. I quickly crumpled the towel and stuffed it in my back pocket. I glanced around to see if I could catch anybody watching me. No luck. I'd never ask Pascoe. What if it was true? I hate to admit it, but that note got to me. I think about it more than I ever should.

"Let's the three of us stop by Champagne Charlie's," I said to Pascoe and Martinez in the locker room. "We can pound a few Bud and eyeball the strippers. There's a new one since you guys have been out of town. You should see the fucking contortions she goes through. Someone there said she licks her own pussy during the midnight show."

"I thought you had this red-hot date," said Pascoe.

"Fuck her," I said. "Let her wait. They like you better if you treat them like shit."

We headed off, three abreast, just like old times. Me in the center, Pascoe to my left, Martinez linked to my right arm.

"Just like a fucking airplane," I said, walking fast, watching pedestrians part or move aside to let us pass.

"Punchline!" I shouted, as we loped along. "So I stood up, tried to kick my ass, missed, fell off the roof, and broke my leg."

Pascoe laughed. Martinez grinned foolishly.

"The nun had a straight razor in her bra," said Pascoe, the bluish streetlights reflecting off his teeth.

"Fucking, right on," I said.

We swaggered into Champagne Charlie's, got seats at the counter, right in front of the stage, ordered a round of Bud, and settled in.

"This Canadian beer tastes like gopher piss," I said, drawing a few ugly stares from the other customers. But we knocked back three each anyway.

The stripper was named La Velvet and was very tall and black. She took a liking to Pascoe, winked, and crinkled her nose at him as she did the preliminary shedding of clothes. When she was naked except for red high-heeled shoes, she dragged her ass around the stage like a cat in heat. Then, facing us, with her hands flat on the floor at her sides, she edged toward us, braced her heels on the carpet at the edge of the stage, spreading her legs wide until her pussy was about a foot from Pascoe's face.

"Way to go, baby," I yelled. "Hey, Marty, how'd you like to eat that for breakfast? And lunch? And dinner?"

Martinez grinned amiably, pretending to understand.

I stood up and clapped in rhythm to her gyrating body.

"Behave yourself," hissed Pascoe.

"Way to go, baby. Wrap those long legs around his neck. Show me a guy who won't go down on his lady, and I will."

The bouncer came over and tapped me on the shoulder.

"Sit down," he said.

I was holding a bottle of Bud in my right hand. For half a second I considered smashing it across his face. He was obviously an ex-fighter, with a nose several times broken and heavy scar tissue across his eyebrows. Then I felt Pascoe's huge hand on my arm.

"Sit down, Barry," he growled. "Why do you always have to act like an asshole, man? Why do you have to be bigger and tougher and raunchier and more rough-and-ready than everybody else?"

I sat down. La Velvet was gathering up her robe and heading down some stairs at the back of the stage. I noticed that her nails were painted a deep, dark red, the color of a ripe cherry.

"Sorry, I just get carried away," I said lamely.

Pascoe glared at me.

"You spoiled my chances, man. Why do you have to act like a fucking animal?"

I didn't have any answer for him. I suppose I could blame it on the summer, the pressure of playing pro ball, being a long way from home for the first time.

La Velvet, wrapped in a scarlet robe that matched her high heels, appeared from a door on Martinez's side of the counter. As she walked behind us she leaned close to Pascoe and said in a throaty voice, "My last show's at midnight. You plannin' to be here?"

"Somebody'd have to kill me to keep me away," said Pascoe, grinning like a maniac.

"Don't you have a date?" he said to me as soon as La Velvet was gone.

"Yeah," I replied.

"You don't seem very excited about it anymore."

"Why don't you guys walk over to the restaurant with me? Just to keep me company."

"Naw, I want to sit here and dream about that midnight show and what's comin' after it," said Pascoe.

"You want to come for a walk, Marty?" I said.

Martinez stared at me, smiling, uncomprehending.

"Walk. Hike. El tromp-tromp. How the hell do you say *walk* in Spanish?"

Martinez continued to look confused. He glanced from me to Pascoe, as if seeking advice.

"Walk with me!" I howled, standing up, my beer bottle clutched in my hand. Out of the corner of my eye I could see the bouncer start in our direction.

"Behave yourself," said Pascoe urgently, standing up, too. "We'll come with you, just stop acting like a jerk." To the bouncer he said,

"We're just leaving. Two drinks and my buddy here thinks he's Tarzan."

"Pound that Bud," I called out as Pascoe pulled me toward the exit. People were staring at us as we made our way across the nightclub and up the stairs to the street.

The movies were just out and Granville Street was teeming as we walked along three abreast, arms linked. I forged ahead, the point of the wedge, the pilot. Pascoe relived that night's game, every at-bat, every play he was involved in.

"Man, if I'd just laid back and waited for the slider," he was saying. "He struck me out with an off-speed slider because I was guessing fast ball —"

"Punchline!" I shouted. "If you can get up and go to work, the leasht I can do ith pack you a lunch."

I guffawed loudly. Martinez grinned, jigging along beside me. Pascoe, however, continued to analyze the game.

As we rolled along, we passed the shadowy entrance to the King's Castle. One door was open, but it was too dark to see inside. A fan expelled the odors of warm beer and cigarette smoke onto the sidewalk. There were several men in the entranceway. Two of them stood near the doorway, touching, talking earnestly into each other's faces. Pascoe talked on, looking neither right nor left. A tawny-skinned young man in tight Levis, his white shirt open, tied in a knot across his belly, leaned insolently against a wall.

"Fucking queers," I yelled, pushing on faster.

"Behave yourself," snapped Pascoe.

Beyond the King's Castle I breathed easier. As we were passing, my eyes had flashed across those of the tawny-skinned boy and I had felt that he knew. As I know. That it is not a matter of will I or won't I, but only of how long before I do.

"Punchline!" I wailed. "Trouble was, the pilot was gay."

"Ha, ha," cried Martinez, thinking he understood.

The
Eddie Scissons Syndrome

I COULD HAVE BEEN another Greg Luzinski. A sportswriter wrote about me that I run forward with the same speed a mixer full of concrete moves backward. I'm built close to the ground; my teammates used to call me Dumpster. Just like the "Bull" I was big and slow, but I could hit the ball a mile with great regularity.

Last spring, when I was a junior in college, there were scouts from twelve of the fourteen American League teams out to look at me play during the zone playoffs in Tampa. We didn't get to the College World Series, weren't expected to, that's why the scouts were there for the preliminaries. I was the most exciting designated-hitter prospect they'd seen in a few seasons. I batted .481 in three playoff games before we were eliminated, and four of those hits were home runs.

I had it made. But what did I know? A stupid kid. I'd been an all-American in football in high school. I played center. So, just to keep in shape, last fall, hardly a year ago, I worked out with the football team even though I'd been warned not to. But I was indestructible. I was Lawrence "Dumpster" Kavanagh, future baseball superstar, with one more year of college, five or six hundred home runs, and a few million dollars on the horizon. Until I took a block directly on my right knee, a block that shattered everything that can shatter in a knee. I've had five operations and been poked and probed by the best doctors in the United States, but I'll wear a brace until I die, and the idea of playing professional baseball now comes under the heading, "What Might Have Been."

"Just be thankful you've always been an A student," my baseball coach said to me. He was as heartbroken as I was because we'd become good friends and he was gonna be my agent. He was the guy who warned me the most often and loudest about staying away from the football field. But what did I know? He's been a real friend and never once said I told you so, though he should have, and we'd probably both have felt better if he had.

Once I was off the baseball team, my scholarship gone forever, just like my knee ligaments, there was never any question of my not staying in school. To meet tuition I ended up working as a teaching and research assistant, read general gofer, for Professor Eugene Willis, who taught sports psychology, which was my major. Willis knew his stuff, but he was a devil for detail, a tall, balding man with a gimlet stare and a reputation for being demanding and bad-tempered. Behind his back, me and the other students called him Professor Nit-picker.

"You can call me Larry," I said when I went to his office after I'd been assigned to him. "Actually everybody calls me Dumpster. Feel free."

"Lawrence will be quite satisfactory, old man," he said. Professor Willis was delicately built, with long, thin wrists that dangled loosely from the sleeves of his jacket. He could have been anywhere from thirty-five to fifty. He looked youthful, but he had crow's feet at the corners of his eyes, and I noticed that the veins stood out on the backs of his hands. He had sunken cheeks, though his lips were very red and perpetually puckered. I'd been planning to ask if he was Gene or Eugene.

"No need for you to call me Doctor," he said. "Professor Willis will suffice."

To think I actually applied to work with this guy, I thought. I'd never taken a class from him, but he was doing a study on something I was really interested in, an aspect of sports psychology having to do with sports impostors, people who lie about having played professional sports, lie until they believe their own lies. I thought of Willis's reputation of being a petulant time-waster in faculty and committee meetings. He was said to be pernicious when it came to procedural rules and had been known to criticize and pick at female faculty members until they rushed in tears from departmental meetings.

I weighed Willis's bad temper and accountant mentality against several brilliant articles he had produced for learned journals, and decided I could learn a great deal from him. I would simply try to stay on his good side. Besides, as anyone connected with a university knows, a teaching assistant's only purpose in life is to do as he's told, or as one of my fellow researchers said, "To have a bowel movement any time your professor says 'shit.'"

Willis named the phenomenon he was studying The Eddie Scissons Syndrome. The idea for the study and the name for it derived from a piece of fiction. A few years ago there was a novel about baseball called *Shoeless Joe,* in which a character named Eddie Scissons, an eighty-nine-year-old man, claimed to be the oldest living Chicago Cub. He claimed to have been a relief pitcher for the Cubs in the years 1908 to 1910, the era of Tinker-to-Evers-to-Chance. Eddie Scissons told a convincing story, but it turned out he was a stone-cold liar who had never played major-league baseball. Eddie Scissons had simply started telling a few little lies about a major-league career, but they got larger and more elaborate as time passed. Eventually he came to believe the lies and was sometimes surprised when people who knew the truth, like his daughters, pointed out his falsehoods to him.

Professor Willis was impressed by the book. He actually tracked down the author at some university town in Iowa and discovered that Eddie Scissons was based on a real character, though his name had been changed in the book. Professor Willis began to wonder how many guys like Eddie Scissons were out there, how many old men, all across America, were lying through their teeth every time they talked of their careers in the big leagues.

"Until the mid-seventies it was easy for this type of sports impostor to get away with it," Professor Willis explained to me. "As long as they didn't claim to have been stars, as long as they didn't meet with a player from the team or the era they were lying about — who was going to call them on it? But then came *The Baseball Encyclopedia,* a complete statistical record of anybody who ever even had their nose on a major-league ballfield. A visit to the reference department of any public library will quickly confirm or deny any story you might hear. In a way it's sad. Over the next twenty or twenty-five years, the existence of *The Baseball Encyclopedia* will become general knowledge, and this particular variety of sports impostor will all but disappear. All that will be left will be the pathological liars who don't care in the least whether or not they are found out. The more canny liars will have to switch to tennis, football, or golf, where the statistics aren't so well documented."

I told Professor Willis about my brush with an impostor once when I was visiting Los Angeles. I'd spent the night in a cheap, old hotel and was about to take a cab to the bus depot, when a seedy old man carrying a dirty brindled suitcase said he was also going to the bus depot and asked to share the cab.

We were no sooner settled, me in the back, the old man beside the driver, when the old man began talking.

"I bet you don't know who I am," he said to the driver, obviously proud of what he was about to reveal.

I wondered who he could possibly be that would mean anything to me or the stolid black man who was driving the cab. The old man was about sixty-five, slim in the way years of serious drinking slim a man. His fingers were stained with nicotine. He wore a shabby suit with a World War II veteran's button on the lapel.

"I bet I don't," said the driver good-naturedly, eyeing the man.

"How about you, son?" the old man said, turning toward me.

I shook my head.

"Do you fellas ever go to the movies?"

"Not much," said the driver.

"I do," I said.

"Old movies?" said the man, again turning toward me.

"Sure. I like to watch the late shows."

"Me too," said the driver.

"Then don't you recognize this profile?" the man said, touching his cheek with a stained finger, his eyes glowing with pride.

I expected him to claim that he had been a bit player in old films, and he could have gotten away with that. Instead, he smiled more excitedly and said, "I'm Pat O'Brien."

The driver just grunted.

There was no way this derelict could ever have been Pat O'Brien, even if the real Pat O'Brien had fallen on the hardest of times. For one thing, I knew Pat O'Brien was at least fifteen years older, shorter, and of a stockier build. But I decided to play along.

"Well, it's a pleasure to meet you, Mr. O'Brien," I said, and reached over the seat and shook his dry, thin hand.

The cab pulled up at the bus depot. I paid my share of the fare and hurried away because I didn't want to listen to any more lies. I could see he was dying to elaborate about his career now that he had an audience. The old man was busy digging in the pockets of his soiled suit for change. I heard the cab driver say as he handed the man his suitcase, "I would have taken Pat O'Brien for a bigger tipper."

The idea of impostors fascinated me, and I was excited about helping Professor Willis research his study.

"I first developed an interest in plain, everyday impostors," Professor Willis told me, "after a colleague of mine admitted he was a classic example of an impostor who was not a con man. He simply embellished a story little by little over the years until he suddenly realized one day that he was an out-and-out liar. He was able to see what he had done and was even able to understand why he had done it. Most of the people we'll be investigating won't be blessed with such insight.

"My colleague was stationed in the Pacific during the latter days of World War II, only a few miles away from the base where the *Enola Gay* took off for Japan on her mission of destruction. At first, he told the truth; then he moved himself to that base. Later he claimed to have handled the documents clearing the *Enola Gay* for her mission. Next he claimed to have been part of the ground crew. Then he stated that he personally loaded the bomb into her hold. The next step was to claim to have ridden along in the *Enola Gay* as an observer. Finally he embellished the story to where he was a part of the actual crew of the *Enola Gay*. He said it got to the point where he lived in fear that he would meet somebody who knew or had been part of the real crew. He went on telling the story until one day he suddenly realized that he didn't like living in fear of being found out. He didn't confess, but simply dropped all mention of the situation and if someone brought it up he would say, 'I'm afraid I've been inclined to exaggerate the importance of my role. I suggest you look up the historical accounts. My experience has been that history tends to expand, like water seeping into a vat of dry beans.' "

Professor Willis used a chunk of his grant money to run ads in sports magazines, and everything from *The New Yorker* to the *National Enquirer* to sleazy soldier-of-fortune magazines. We spent several hours composing the ads, making them oblique enough so no one would suspect our true purpose. The ads simply asked to hear from ex–major-league baseball players, as well as relatives or friends of ex–major leaguers.

We got more replies than we ever anticipated. Only a handful of ex–big leaguers replied in person, but we got hundreds of letters from fans and acquaintances who had spent a few hours or a few minutes with some famous player. There were a few letters from grandchildren, neighbors, even an ex-wife or two. We checked the names in *The Baseball Encyclopedia*, when neither of us had heard them. We flipped the pages quickly, hoping the name wouldn't be there. And in twelve cases it wasn't. Those were the ones we put aside to follow up on.

One resided in Canada. A worker at the Inco smelter in Sudbury,

Ontario, claimed to have been a relief pitcher for the New York Yankees in 1948 and '49. The woman who wrote to us was a real fan of the impostor. She hadn't known him at the time but was able to name his teammates. There was, of course, no record that the impostor had ever appeared in the big leagues. We didn't check minor-league statistics because our only interest was in major-league impostors.

Another phony story came in the form of a long letter from a friend of a friend of a guy who claimed to be a great minor-league pitcher who, because the major-league teams that at various times owned his contract were overstocked with stars, languished in Triple A for eight years before getting a shot at the Bigs. The letter went on to tell how the player failed because he was too old, his best years given to being a star in the minors. The ex-ballplayer had obviously told this story often, for his voice came through loud and clear, above the voice of the letter writer. However, when we checked the records the erstwhile star from Triple A had never played an inning in the major leagues, though he may indeed have attended spring training. His file was set aside for later investigation.

The most intriguing letter came from a doctor in Columbia, South Carolina. He had a patient, he explained, a ninety-four-year-old man, who had a fantastic but believable story to tell of playing for and being betrayed by the 1917 Chicago White Sox.

"I have no way of verifying my patient's story, though I find him truthful in other matters, and he appears to be in control of his mental faculties in spite of his advanced years. His physical condition is another matter. He suffers from a variety of ailments, the most serious being a disabling heart condition. Any of several ailments could cause his death at any time."

Here, condensed, is the story the old man, Charles Jefferson Kiley, told his doctor.

"I was a catcher by profession. I was born in Jefferson Mills, S.C., in 1889. My mother was black, my father unknown, but certainly a white man, for I was able to 'pass' from an early age. In 1907 I went North and kicked around in various commercial and unorganized minor baseball leagues in Illinois and Ohio. If anyone questioned my ancestry, which only happened when I played badly, I claimed to be an Indian. In fact I played under the name of Chief Kiley and Chief Kelly in a number of towns. I even played for the Chicago American Giants in the Negro League in 1914 or '15, as Chief Kelly.

"In the spring of 1917 I was playing in a commercial league in Chicago when the Sox regular catcher, Ray Schalk, was injured. Mr. Charles Comiskey himself signed me up as a replacement. I played one circuit of the American League, maybe twenty-five or thirty games. I played one series of games against each of the other teams in the league.

"It seems to me that Ray Schalk's recovery and Mr. Comiskey's finding out about my ancestry came about at the same time. I know I don't show in baseball records anywhere, but that is because Mr. Comiskey himself destroyed my records. I wrote to the Chicago White Sox about twenty years ago, and they stated that no one by the name of Charles or Chief Kiley had ever played for them."

The old man, as quoted by his doctor, went on to name several players who were his teammates and recall details of games he played in.

"This one certainly looks promising," said Professor Willis. "If he's a fraud, he's a grand fraud. If he's legitimate, we have some history on our hands. There were occasional black players in the early years of baseball, players who were sneaked in because of their ability, but none as late as 1917. So if he's telling the truth . . ." and Professor Willis came as close to a full smile as he had since I had known him.

"Also, wouldn't it be a coup for us if we could authenticate this man's story and at the same time discredit that tyrant Comiskey? The point that rings so true is the bit about Comiskey personally destroying Kiley's records. It's a known fact that Comiskey's hands were dirty in one way or another almost all his career. If he hadn't been such a petty tyrant, such a cheapskate; if he hadn't defrauded Eddie Cicotte, there wouldn't have been a Black Sox Scandal in 1919. I think we'd better check this one out in person, Lawrence. I want to meet Mr. Kiley."

"I know how we can partially check his story," I said. "Comiskey can destroy all the records he wants from his own files, and he can have withheld information from Cooperstown and *The Baseball Encyclopedia*, but the Chicago newspapers will have carried box scores of all the games. They'll be on microfilm. Maybe one of us should go to Chicago first."

"No. I think we're on to something," said Professor Willis, rubbing his long, dry hands together. "I want to talk to this man in person, get his story down on tape.

"I want you to accompany me on this excursion, Lawrence." Professor Willis was one of those people who talks with a slight English accent, even though he was raised in Cincinnati and had never been outside the U.S. except for brief holidays.

"That's mighty nice of you, Professor." And I guess it was.

He used some of his grant money to fly both of us to Columbia, South Carolina. We took a taxi to the V.A. Hospital on Devine Street, where we had an appointment to meet with Dr. Yeager, the man who wrote us. The hospital grounds were like a park. Beds of iridescent iris sat like ponds on the manicured lawns; the air was scented by yellow jessamine. Virginal white dogwoods were in bloom all along the miles of curving driveways, which were lined with light poles topped by gooseneck lamps, the globes of which reflected violet as the irises, even in midafternoon. The lampposts were of the breakaway variety, designed to be easily dislodged on impact. I noticed that one of the posts had been knocked down; it stretched out on the sunshine-covered grass like the leg of some prehistoric bird. The post had one large dent and was stained at point of impact by blood-red paint. A few shards of headlight glass lay glittering on the pavement and lawn. At the point where the pole was uprooted were dozens of red, blue, and yellow electric wires, exposed like severed muscles.

Dr. Yeager was waiting for us in his office. He was in his mid-fifties, a portly gentleman wearing a brown suit and necktie. He wore large, thick, gold-rimmed glasses. His cheeks looked as if he had just come in from skating on a brisk winter afternoon.

"I'm afraid I'm not much of a baseball fan," Dr. Yeager said after we were comfortably settled in his office. "Oh, I watch a few innings at World Series time, but I'm not knowledgeable enough to vouch for Mr. Kiley's story, except that he seems honest. I'm a devotee of mystery fiction, which I suppose explains why I wrote you. A chance to be a participant in the unraveling of a good mystery, you know.

"I've told Mr. Kiley you were coming," the doctor went on. "He's very excited about it. 'Gives me something to live for,' he says. One of his daughters came in a while ago and spruced him up some."

For his age, Mr. Kiley looked pretty good. He was sitting up in his bed wearing a maroon velvet robe over his hospital gown. He was frail and had never been a large man — five foot seven would be my guess. He had a full head of gray, kinky hair; his complexion was dark, but he certainly did not appear to be black. His eyes were an off-gray, had almost a pewter hue to them.

Professor Willis and I set up our tape recorder. I had worried a bit about how Professor Willis would act; he had been irritable and sarcastic with me on many occasions, showing a general contempt for our subjects which I found disturbing. Mr. Kiley was nervous at first and kept staring at the recorder, but Professor Willis relaxed him by keeping the conversation general for the first few minutes. In a soft, but heavily Southern, accent, Mr. Kiley, with some prompting from Professor Willis, told the same story the doctor had related earlier. He stopped frequently to clear his throat, laughed a few times, seeming pleased with the accuracy and detail of his own recall.

"It was that fellow Comiskey," said Mr. Kiley. "I bet he knew all along about my being a black man. He needed a catcher and he weren't particular where he got one. But he dropped me like I was hot the second Ray Schalk recovered.

"You know, it was old Pants Rowland, the manager, who gave me my walking papers. I went up to the offices of the White Sox and asked to talk to Mr. Comiskey. There was a wooden screen across the window to the office, and this little bald accountant told me to go on my way. Was real snotty to me. When I insisted on speaking to Mr. Comiskey he slammed down that wooden shutter and left me standing alone in the dark hallway."

Mr. Kiley sat back, laughed good-naturedly, looking satisfied with himself.

"Excuse us a minute," I said, and shut off the recorder.

Professor Willis and I conferred in the corner for a moment.

"That's almost word for word the story of what happened to Joe Jackson in 1919 when he tried to turn in the payoff money he'd received from players involved in the Black Sox Scandal."

"I know," said Professor Willis, and smiled with his fleshy little mouth. "Leave him to me."

"Sorry for the delay, Mr. Kiley," said Professor Willis. "Just a fact or two we had to confirm. You understand."

The old man had apparently dozed off in the minute we were away.

"Charles Comiskey!" he said, his head snapping up, his eyes unfocused.

Dr. Yeager stepped forward, and, waving us aside, took Kiley's pulse. Satisfied, he nodded for us to continue.

"Now, what I want to do is go over the roster of the 1917 White Sox, the people you played with . . ." Professor Willis went down the line-up, Gandil, Collins, Risberg, Weaver. He stuck to easy generalities until he got to the pitching staff.

"I guess you'll always remember catching Dauntless Dave Danforth," he said. The old man chuckled. "First right-hander to use the knuckle ball, they say," Professor Willis continued. "Ray Schalk once wrapped his mitt in a blanket in order to catch him. Did you have much trouble handling his knuckler?" and the professor smiled amiably.

"I managed," Kiley said, a little uneasily. "Stopped most of them with my body though."

"And how about Frank Shellenback? Dr. Yeager says Frank Shellenback was your roommate. As good a southpaw as ever played the game. Too bad about his accident. I suppose you kept in touch with him over the years."

"Oh, yes, yes," said the old man. "My roommate . . ." his eyes were staring at the wall behind us. I glanced out the window where the flower beds shimmered in the sunlight. I could see the damaged lamppost lying like a reversed question mark on the velvety lawn.

"Frank Shellenback was your roommate, wasn't he?" Professor Willis pressed.

"Oh, yes, sure he was. Charles Comiskey. It was Charles Comiskey tore up my records so nobody'd ever know I played in the Bigs."

"Mr. Kiley, I think it's time we got down to some facts." Professor Willis's voice took on the whining edge he sometimes used in classes after a student gave a particularly uninformed answer. "Dauntless Dave Danforth was a southpaw. To my knowledge he never threw a knuckle ball in his life. Frank Shellenback didn't come to the White Sox until 1918 so you couldn't have caught him and he couldn't have been your roommate. And I don't know of any accident."

The old man stared around wildly, his eyes lighting on Dr. Yeager.

"You said Doc told you about my roommate. I thought —"

"I lied," said Professor Willis. "Did you ever play for the White Sox, Mr. Kiley? Tell the truth!"

"Of course I did. It was Charles Comiskey who —"

"Name some of the men who batted against you!"

"Well . . . there was Joe Jackson. Shoeless Joe he was called." Mr. Kiley was sweating now. Dr. Yeager was inching toward the bed as if getting ready to step between the old man and the professor.

"Joe Jackson was on your team," Professor Willis said loudly.

"Oh, well . . . there was Bill Dickey with the Yankees." He paused for a moment, his brow furrowed. "Rogers Hornsby . . . and Charlie Grimm —"

"Wrong on all counts," thundered the professor. "Bill Dickey didn't even come into the league until 1928. Hornsby played in the National League. So did Grimm. Grimm wasn't even playing in the majors in 1917. You know what I did before we came here, Mr. Kiley? I wrote away to the *Chicago Tribune* and I got the box scores of White Sox games for the two months you claim to have played. Charles Comiskey couldn't destroy the back issues of the *Chicago Tribune*. You never played a day of major-league baseball in your life!"

Professor Willis's face was now as red as Dr. Yeager's. Professor Willis moved closer to the old man, his mouth snapping out words, his fleshy lips like red meat in the old man's face.

"I wanted to see what a stone-cold, conniving liar looked like. I wanted to get down your lies on tape for everyone to hear."

The old man shrunk into his pillows; he covered one ear with a hand, but seemed to lack the strength to cover the other.

"I think you've done quite enough," Dr. Yeager said to the professor.

"Admit you're a fraud!" Professor Willis shouted. "I want to hear you admit it."

The old man remained silent, his face gray.

"I'm sorry," I said, addressing both Mr. Kiley and the doctor. Neither gave any indication of hearing me.

"You have to leave now," Dr. Yeager was saying.

"Admit it! We spent good money to fly here."

"Leave the man his dignity!" I shouted, and grabbing Professor Willis by the shoulders propelled him unwillingly into the hall.

"Pathological liar," he was saying. "He's probably not a veteran either; he's probably not black. Pathological —"

"Why didn't you tell me what you knew," I shouted. "There was no reason to come here except to humiliate him. I don't want to be part of this kind of thing."

"What kind of thing?" demanded Professor Willis, his eyes bugging, his chest heaving. "Frauds deserve no pity. Liars, frauds —"

I gave him a hard push and he expelled air sharply as his back came in contact with the wall.

I snatched up a pillow off a gurney in the corridor and stalked off down the hall. As I passed the door to Mr. Kiley's room I could see Dr. Yeager bending over his patient. Fluorescent light glinted off the doctor's glasses.

"Lawrence! Gather up the equipment!" Professor Willis shouted after me. My heart felt like a basketball being dribbled. I was furious not only at what Willis had done to the old man, but at his making me a part of it.

"That's an order! Lawrence! Dumpster! Dumpster!" he called after me. I didn't turn or look back at all.

On the hospital steps, the brilliant sunlight seemed to spotlight me as I stared about disoriented, blinking as if I had just emerged from a movie.

As I stood on the steps I glanced down at the pillow I was carrying and realized that I had made a decision as to what to do when I was still inside the building. I made my way down the wide, sun-bleached stairs to the road. I stared down the long, gently curving driveway to where an occasional car spun past on the main street. There were about fifteen light poles between me and Devine Street.

I placed the pillow over my right shoulder to protect my collar-bone. I took a short run and hit the first post low and hard, a tough, clean block, just as if I were back on the football field taking out an opposing lineman. The pole snapped from its mooring and toppled across the sunshine-bright grass. It hit so softly the glass of the light standard didn't even break.

I had to take two runs at the second one before it dislodged and fell like thunder on the pavement, the iris-colored glass showering up from the concrete. As I disengaged the third post, something snapped in my shoulder. After the next one my knee was throbbing like a toothache.

I could hear shouting voices behind me, feet pounding heavily on the pavement. I switched the pillow to my left shoulder, increased my running speed. Another pole toppled onto the road, glass fragments skittering crazily. If I hit each remaining pole squarely, I could finish the row and be at Devine Street before my pursuers caught up with me.

Diehard

For Denny Boyd

I REMEMBER good old Herky saying many a time, "The only way to kill an old catcher is to cut off his head and then hide it." We'd always laugh, even if it was the hundredth time over the years that Herky had said it to me. We'd laugh, me and Herky, and whoever else was around the big table at Bronko's Polish Falcon Bar. Bronko's ain't the Hyatt Regency, if you know what I mean. But then, Superior, Wisconsin, ain't San Francisco, and me and Herky and the boys at Bronko's Polish Falcon ain't lawyer and stockbroker types, so it all evens out.

Herky grew up right here in East Superior, not a dozen blocks from Bronko's. He was German. Arnold Waldemar Herkheiser was his full handle. The house where he grew up still stands, a sad, old two-story place, covered in imitation brick the gray sooty color of a melting snowbank.

When we came home in the fall from our first year in Triple A baseball, Herky married Stella Piska, who lived next door to St. Wenceslaus Church there on Fourth Street. The year Herky hit the Bigs for the first time, him and Stella bought the old Wasylinski place, right after the old folks had to go into a nursing home. I helped Stella and Herky clean the junk out of that little house: tons and tons of Polish newspapers, *Life* magazines, *Collier's*, and *Saturday Evening Posts* by the hundreds. The whole second bedroom was stacked right to the ceiling, and the basement was stuffed full, some magazines stacked so close to the furnace it was a wonder the place hadn't burned down years before.

Stella still lives there. Their kids are married now; the girl lives in Seattle, the boy in Minneapolis. I've always been half in love with Stella, and, what with my Margie bein' gone for goin' on four years now, I figure after a decent period of time I'll propose to Stella. I figure we can have a pleasant old age together. But that's the future. What we got here is a problem in the present: what to do with Herky's ashes.

The service was at St. Wenceslaus yesterday. There was a viewing time down at Borowski's Funeral Home on Tuesday night. They'd laid Herky out real nice. He looked good, his silver hair combed up in a big pompadour, the way he liked, that broken beak of his about a half inch to starboard, the way it had been since he slid into Sherm Lollar's knee at third base in, what would it have been, the '44 season? And his hands, those big mitts of his, were resting on his belly; at one time or another he must have broke every knuckle he owned. The first time I cried for Herky was when I looked at those great, scarred hands, the right thumbnail split down the middle, ridged like the peak of a roof. I knew I was crying for me as much as for Herky. I'd lost a friend I'd known all my sixty-two years.

Stella had laid out Herky's catching gear on the bottom half of the coffin. Pretty cruddy stuff compared to what catchers have today, the thin shin guards, the small mask, the old cowhide mitt the size of a plate with a round indentation in the middle. It added a nice touch. The Red Sox remembered and sent their Midwest scout to the funeral — a classy organization. Walt Dropo and Mel Parnell, teammates of ours on the Red Sox, came, and Swede Tenholm drove down from Hibbing, Minnesota, where he manages a mine there in the Iron Range.

"Geez, Hector, he looks better than you do," the other old

ballplayers said to me, after viewing the body. "All you'd have to do is lie down and we could have a double funeral," said Swede.

They kidded me some more about my playing days. I'd been a good fielding, no-hit, infielder for four seasons with the Red Sox. I put in five more years in the minors; in those days you could play your way up and down in the minor leagues. Now, if you're not a true major-league prospect, you're driving a truck by the time you're twenty-five.

We went back to Stella's after the service. Neighbors brought tons of food, and the place was crowded. The living room seemed so small. Nobody sat in Herky's chair, that square box of a chair covered in maroon velvet with a raised leaf pattern, ferns in concentric swirls. Both arms of the chair were worn bald from Herky always hanging first one leg and then the other over the sides. There were food stains, grease, and beer-can rings on the arms and seat cushion of that chair. Stella furnished the rest of the room at least three times over the years but Herky's chair dated back to when they got married, 1943. He was twenty, Stella was eighteen. The wedding picture hangs in the dining room, right above the silver chest on the buffet. I swear we were never that young: me and Herky, fresh-faced, our hair brush-cut and watered; Herky's brother in his Marine uniform; Stella not as good-looking as she is now, all sharp angles and frizzy hair, made almost ugly by the wartime women's fashions.

The children and grandchildren said their good-byes. The son and his family would take the sister to Minneapolis for a day before she flew home to Seattle. The neighbors trickled away one family at a time, with much hugging and reassuring. Stella and I were left alone.

We sat at the kitchen table drinking coffee laced with Irish whiskey — Old Tennis Shoes, as Herky called it. Herky's ashes sat across the room on the kitchen counter, amid cake boxes and plates of sandwiches draped in wax paper. Borowski the undertaker had said, "Why don't you drop over next week and pick up the ashes," but Stella insisted she wanted them that day. Borowski delivered them himself, early that evening.

We had several drinks, mainly in silence, the kind of silence life-long friends share with comfort. Finally, it was Stella who looked over to where the blue, long-necked urn sat like a heron among rocks.

"What should I do?" she asked.

"Some women keep their husband's ashes on the mantelpiece, or in their bedroom." Stella shook her head. The attic? The basement? The garage? At each suggestion Stella continued to shake her head gently.

"I don't have any desire to keep them. They're not Herky. I've got my memories here inside me." She patted her dress just below her breasts. Stella's yellow hair is graying now, her face is thinner, her eyes sharper. But she's still a beautiful woman. "I think it's sad to keep something like that," she went on. "It's the kind of thing dreary old movie has-beens do to seek sympathy."

"I could scatter them the next time I go for a walk," I said. "Herky and I must have walked the tracks and the trestle out by the flour mill a thousand miles or more. That was his favorite place in the world, walking across the trestle looking down at the fields of marsh grass, especially if the moon was out and glinted off the tracks and the water in the grass."

"It's an idea," said Stella, "but I'd like something special, some-place special."

Though both Herky and me played for the Boston Red Sox, once our playing days were over we were never more than interested fans. We followed the standings in the newspapers and watched the "Game of the Week" on Saturday, but we didn't have the money to travel to Boston. In fact, neither of us were ever back there again. We went down to Milwaukee once in a while, but we mainly watched minor-league baseball until 1960, when the Minnesota Twins came into being.

On Saturdays and Sundays we could jump in the car right after breakfast and get to Met Stadium in time for batting practice. The four of us took hundreds and hundreds of trips down Interstate 35 to the Twin Cities. The Met was a lot like Fenway Park, a solid, friendly stadium with natural grass and open spaces. We even bought season tickets one year, but it proved too much for us, getting home at two A.M. and having to get up to go to work, then drive back to Minneapolis the next night, sometimes not arriving until the second or third inning. But what a season it was. That magical year when Minnesota won their only pennant. We went to the World Series, and it was more exciting than playing in one. Both Herky and I were with the Red Sox in 1946 when we lost to the Cardinals and Harry Brecheen in seven games. Herky caught two of those games and I got to pinch hit twice, 0–2, and play three innings as a substitute second baseman.

The Season. The Season was what we called that year. If any one of us mentioned the Season, we all knew it was 1965, the year the Twins went to the World Series.

They were 102–60, first by seven games over the White Sox. Sam Mele was manager. And they had Don Mincher, Harmon Killebrew, Tony Oliva, Frank Quilici, Zoilo Versalles. Earl Battey was the catcher. Jimmie Hall hit like crazy; he never had another good season.

And the pitchers: Mudcat Grant, Jim Kaat, Jim Perry, and Camilo Pascual at 9–3 had the best percentage year, .750, in his eighteen-year career.

Oh, we loved those Twins. Sometimes after a game we'd go down to the clubhouse, and Herky would talk catching with Earl Battey.

Then there was the series. Los Angeles had such pitching. Tony Oliva, the American League batting champion, hit only .192, poor Earl Battey was at .120, Don Mincher, .130. Only Killebrew and Versalles were able to hit. But the Twins took them to seven games anyway. Jim Kaat against Sandy Koufax.

The seventh game! Two lousy runs!

"Two runs," Herky would cry, and he'd actually have tears in his eyes. "Two runs away from the world championship."

We were disappointed but not bitter. It was just that Koufax was so good. Herky would shake his head and marvel at the speed of his fast ball, the fade of the curve.

"What a joy it would be to be rooting for him instead of against him," Herky said.

"Stella," I said, after maybe the fourth Irish Coffee, "I just thought of something. You know, Herky and me never talked about his dying. I wish we could have. If we could have talked about death we could have really said good-bye." As I said that I thought of Herky, pale as his white hospital shirt, too weak to raise his head from the pillow.

"I know," said Stella. "We didn't talk about it either."

"One thing I remember, Stell, was a night at the Met in Minneapolis. It was one of those perfect baseball nights, the air was soft and warm. There wasn't a hint of a breeze. When we looked up past the blaze of floodlights, the stars winked silver and gold, like bits of tinsel floating in ink. The Twins were winning; all was right with the world. Herky leaned over and said to me, "You know, Hec, if there's anything after this life, the first words I want to hear when I wake up are 'Play ball!' That's the closest we ever came to having a talk about *life*."

"We lived it, Hec," said Stella. "We didn't have to talk about it."

"What I was thinkin', Stell, was maybe the stadium, you know, the Met. Maybe all across the outfield. I'm sure that would make Herky feel good."

"But they're gonna tear the Met down in a couple of years. Soon as the new stadium is ready."

Stella was right. They were just getting started on the new stadium. They'd play both football and baseball there. It was going to be enclosed. There'd been a lot of controversy, letters to the editor and such, because a lot of people hated the idea of an enclosed stadium. But Herky had been philosophical about it.

"I've caught games in snowstorms in April and May. I've seen a whole week of games rained out at the Met. I've seen football games played in a blizzard, the field frozen hard as concrete. We need both kinds of stadium, not that it will ever happen. When the weather's warm and sweet and perfect, play at the Met, but move inside when the weather is terrible.

"You know what's gonna happen, Hec? In a few years, like thirty or forty, all the stadiums will have retractable roofs. It will be the best of both worlds — green grass, blue skies, but a nice clear dome to keep the rain and wind out."

"What about the new stadium?" I said to Stella. "How about getting Herky a seat behind home plate in the new stadium?"

"I think you've hit on a good one," Stella said, and she reached across the kitchen table and squeezed my hand.

We talked for another hour about the idea. The liquor and our emotional exhaustion after the funeral combined to produce a crazy euphoria, a giddiness, like the four of us used to feel sometimes on the long drive home from Minneapolis after a big Twins win. We'd be singing, joking, happy as children. But there were only the two of us now.

"Secrets are so much fun," laughed Stella.

I slept on the sofa, fully clothed.

"You know what my daughter had the nerve to suggest?" Stella had said the night before, just before she went to bed. " 'You know, Mama, now that Daddy's gone, it isn't proper for Hector to stay over, even in the spare room. What will people think?' 'Let them think any damn thing they want,' I said to her. 'I guess Hector's stayed here a few times over the years, so him and your dad could get up at three A.M. to go duck hunting. I stayed at Hector's many a night when poor Margie was dying. If anybody thinks anything about it they can go straight to hell.' "

The letdown the next morning was so solid we could feel it. The sky was low and waxy. Our hangovers had a life of their own. Stella fixed me a big breakfast: fried eggs, toast, bacon, coffee. But all either of us was able to manage was the coffee.

Though we didn't talk about it, we were both wondering if we were doing the right thing. I stopped at my place to change clothes, and I thought of suggesting we rethink our idea. But I could see Stella sitting grimly on the front seat of my car. I took two aspirin and a deep breath and pointed the car toward the interstate and the long drive to the Twin Cities.

We didn't have much to say on the 150 miles to Minneapolis.

Stella sat over by the door, the urn with Herky's ashes sat between us. It was a reverse of the situation when he was alive. Stella always sat in the middle. Whoever owned the car drove, while the other one sat by the window.

I had a difficult time finding a parking spot near to where they were building the new stadium, the Metrodome. Talk was they were gonna name it for that little yap Humphrey. If the Democrats had had a real candidate in 1968, Nixon never would have got elected. I glanced over at Stella. She looked drawn and tired; her face was the same pale color as her hair.

The paved streets were breaking up and were covered in dirt tracked out of the construction site by trucks. It had rained overnight and the streets were slick. We'd both dressed sensibly, me in my green workpants, boots, and a mackinaw, Stella in jeans and a car coat. We walked on past the yellow-lettered sign that said: HARD HATS MUST BE WORN BEYOND THIS POINT.

Cement trucks rumbled by, groaning like dinosaurs. A crane passed back and forth overhead, slabs of concrete dangling from its beak. Finally we heard a voice above the melee shouting, "Hey! Hey!" From a wooden construction shack, a beefy man emerged; he was wearing a red-and-black checkered jacket, steel-toed boots, and a scarred and dented silver hard hat. Stella and I waited for him to catch up to us.

Stella, waving the urn in her left hand, had to yell to be heard. My head ached and listening to the construction noises was like letting someone whittle little pieces off the back of my head with a jackknife.

"I suppose there's nothin' wrong with it," the man said. Then he smiled, a loose-lipped, lopsided smile. "This does give a whole new meaning to a guy saying, 'I'd die for a front-row seat at all the Twins games.' No offense."

"None taken," I said. "He was a real diehard fan of the Twins. There's nothin' Herky would have liked better than a season ticket behind home plate, with nothing foolish like workin' for a living to interrupt his enjoyment of baseball."

"A hell of an idea," the foreman said. "I'm more of a Vikings fan myself. And, by God, if I die before this place is finished I'll have my old lady plant me on the fifty-yard line."

"Where is home plate gonna be?" asked Stella.

The man stopped and stared around him; he looked puzzled for a moment, as if trying to get his bearings.

"Come on back to the shack and we'll look at the blueprints to make sure," he said.

At the shack he fitted each of us with a bulky yellow hard hat with VISITOR stenciled across the crown.

He held the blueprints up to the light, making them look like ghostly writing on a midnight-blue background.

"See, the press box goes here," he said, marking a section with a dirty thumbnail, "so the plate would be here." He pointed out another squiggle on the blueprint.

The three of us picked our way across the muddy site. Cement trucks pregnant with concrete grumbled past us. Stella cradled the indigo urn in the crook of her left arm.

"The first row of seats will be right along here," the foreman said.

The odors of freshly sawed wood, of wet cement, of old fires, filled the air. The cloud cover lightened a bit, and though we still couldn't see the sun, the intensity of light quickened dramatically.

"First row, Hector, what do you think?" said Stella. "An aisle seat. Herky can put his feet on the screen, chug a beer, spill mustard down the front of his shirt while he tries to eat a hot dog, keep score, and tell the catcher how to call the game."

"Looks good to me," I said.

The concrete forms were held together by aluminum-colored industrial staples. The foreman caught the attention of a cement-truck driver heading for a spot fifty yards away. He walked out, and as the truck laboriously backed up, a safety horn bleating annoyingly, he directed it to a standstill next to us. He yanked the spout down and positioned it for pouring.

"You got to put it down if you want us to cover it up," the foreman said.

"Oh, my," said Stella.

The close sky, the raw, chilling air, the confusion about us all took their toll on our resolve.

"There was no place Herky loved more than a ballpark," I said. "Even after they close this one in he'll still have a choice view of Twins games, until long after either of us will care about it anymore."

Stella smiled a wan smile and, leaning over, stared into the dark recesses of the concrete form.

"If you want, this will be our secret," I said. "Tell the kids you did something more conventional."

"Our secret," said Stella, and squeezed my hand.

The foreman banged on the back of the truck, and a slide of concrete rushed into the void. He steered the spout down a six-foot length of form, banged on the truck again, and the flow stopped.

"Now," he said.

I put my arm around Stella's waist; we each gripped the glazed urn. Together we lowered it as deep into the form as our arms would allow. Stella closed her eyes and grimaced as we released it. The urn dropped less than two feet before it met the wet cement.

"Thanks," we said.

The foreman nodded, signaled the truck again, and a second rush of cement was released into the form, filling it to the brim.

"Play ball," I said softly. Then Stella and I picked our way back toward the construction shack and the street.

Searching for Freddy

For Lee

"HE RAN LIKE A GHOST," one old-timer said of Sweet Freddy Schiraldi. "One minute he was stepping stealthily away from first, the next he was at second. Sometimes it seemed like no one saw him stealing. The catcher would just lob the ball back to the pitcher (there would be no infielder covering second base anyway), and Sweet Freddy would already be taking his lead, digging himself a foothold with that special cleat he had on his right shoe, getting ready to zoom toward third."

"People never get tired of reading about the base stealers," said my editor at *Sports Center Magazine*.

"But I get tired of writing about them," I replied. "Henderson, Raines, Coleman, Cangelosi, this season we've done something on each one individually and the four of them collectively. What else is there?"

"Your problem," said the editor. "Find a new angle."

"I've already compared them with Brock and Wills. In fact I interviewed Brock and Wills, got their opinions on each of them."

"Why not go way back?" He ruffled through the dog-eared pages of *The Baseball Encyclopedia*. "Look here! In 1938 Stan Hack led the National League in stolen bases with sixteen. Interview his widow, see what the old speedster thought of Brock and Wills. He's only been dead a few years."

I made a sour face.

"And look at this," he said, leafing backward for several pages. "Who the hell was Freddy Schiraldi? He led the American League in 1931 and '32. He stole over sixty bases each year, in a time when twenty-five was a big deal. Oh! He played for the St. Louis Browns, no wonder I've never heard of him."

"I made a half-assed try at contacting him when Brock was closing in on the record," I said, "but no one knows what became of him. Other sportswriters must have tried over the years."

"The encyclopedia keeps pretty well up to date; they show him as still alive. He was born in 1909, that would make him seventy-seven. I want you to find Freddy Schiraldi, tie him in with the present-day whizzes. Find out from him what it felt like to be years ahead of his time."

There wasn't much to go on. Freddy Schiraldi's entry in *The Baseball Encyclopedia* looked like this:

	G	AB	H	2B	3B	HR	HR %	R	RBI	BB	SO	SB	BA	SA	Pinch Hit AB	Pinch Hit H	G by POS
SCHIRALDI, WILLIAM FRED (Sweet Freddy)																	
Freddy Schiraldi — b. Aug. 3 1909, Jersey City, N.J. BR TR 5'8" 155 lbs.																	
1932 STL A	149	600	189	8	4	7	.06	120	60	75	77	61	.315	.483	1	0	2B-149
1933 STL A	150	581	174	12	4	4	.06	101	65	71	55	65	.299	.473	1	0	2B-150

That was it. Two years as a successful professional, then oblivion. What happened to cut his career so short? Where did he go? Where is he today?

I started out with the obvious. I contacted *The Baseball Encyclopedia*.

"Sorry," said their representative. "He's one of the few who have slipped away from us. He's probably dead, but we've no evidence to that effect. There is a note on his file that says 'Serious medical??' And, oh yeah, skip Cooperstown, we've been in touch with them; they know less than we do."

"Names of next of kin? Anything like that?"

"Wife's name was Mary. Married in 1930. *That* should make him a lot easier to find; can't be all that many women named Mary out there."

"Thanks for your help," I said.

"If you do find him, promise you'll let us know. There've been a lot of inquiries over the years. Everyone has promised to let us know if they find anything."

"Add my promise to the list," I said.

I decided that a logical beginning would be to call all the Schiraldis in the Jersey City phone book, but, I also decided, if someone else had been looking for Freddy, they must have already done that. I checked with a couple of acquaintances in sportswriting.

"Forget it," they said. They had tried during the Wills and Brock years, but Sweet Freddy Schiraldi was a permanently missing person way back then.

There were more Schiraldis in Jersey City than I would have imagined. I called an Anthony Schiraldi. When a male voice answered I said, "My name is Joe McCoy, I'm a sportswriter. I was wondering if you've ever heard of a baseball player named Sweet Freddy Schiraldi?"

"Who is this, man? Are you one of Vito's gorillas?"

"Sweet Freddy Schiraldi," I repeated.

"Listen, Vito knows I'm good for the dough, man. I've just had a run of bad luck."

"Live in fear," I said, and hung up.

It is a nine-hour drive to Jersey City, a place that ranks right up there with Gary, Indiana, and Butte, Montana, as my least favorite places in North America.

A couple of hours in the Jersey City Library going through old telephone books, city directories, and newspapers, and I had an address for an Anthony Schiraldi, shoemaker, and an M. Schiraldi, laborer, the only ones in Jersey City in 1909.

I also found a quotation in the *New York World* of 1933 where someone asked Ty Cobb what he thought of "Flying" Freddy Schiraldi, when it looked, early in the season, like Freddy might challenge Cobb's high of ninety-six steals.

"He floats," said Cobb. "I don't think that young man's feet touch the ground between first and second. That, or he leaves his shadow behind when he runs. I've never seen anyone draw as few throws as he does. The catcher is hardly aware he's stealing until it's too late. And this is only his second season. If he stays healthy he'll easily surpass my lifetime total in a few years."

The building once occupied by Anthony Schiraldi, shoemaker, was now a video store, but the neighborhood was very old, houses and businesses mixed. By making a few inquiries I was put in touch with a ninety-year-old woman who had lived all her life in the district.

"Sure I remember Schiraldi the shoemaker," said the old woman, who was as tiny as a child, dressed in what looked like black umbrella cloth. "How come you want to know about him? He's been dead maybe fifty years."

"I write about baseball," I explained. "I'm interested in finding his son, Freddy."

"What year is this?" the old woman suddenly demanded.

"It's 1986," I replied.

"I thought so," she said. "It's sixty years since Tony Schiraldi died. In 1934, the year my oldest daughter got married, Freddy Schiraldi disappeared. Came home from playing baseball, his leg was ruined. He could barely walk with a crutch. Had running sores all over one of his legs, caused by rotten bones of some kind. Just up and disappeared. He must be long dead."

"Did he have children? Do you know what became of his wife?"

"Why don't you ask her these nosy questions?"

"She's alive, then?"

"We exchange Christmas cards," the old woman said. "She wasn't a local girl, wasn't even Italian as far as I know. She stayed around for a year or so after Freddy disappeared, then went home to Philadelphia."

She produced a black notebook, and I copied down an address for Mary Schiraldi in Germantown, Pennsylvania.

Rogers Hornsby, in one of his last interviews, was asked about great second basemen he had known. "There was a kid played second for the Browns for a couple of years in the thirties; I only saw him play two or three times, but I never saw anyone could steal a base like him. His name was Freddy Schiraldi."

Mary Schiraldi was a tall, thin woman with a sad, kindly smile. Her hair was iron-gray, her shoulders slightly stooped. She lived on the ground floor of a large, old house in a section of Germantown, a Philadelphia suburb. The homes in her area had been elegant at one time, got run down, and were now being occupied by yuppie couples intent on restoring them.

"I've been in this house for fifty years," she said, as we entered the dark living room stuffed with furniture that was old but well cared for. "I've rented rooms, boarded a college student or two from time to time. My needs are small."

I kept my questions general, asking mainly about her remembrances of Freddy as a baseball player. I wanted to leave the personal questions until last, in case they brought up unpleasant memories.

"What kind of injury was it that ended Freddy's career?" I asked.

"Oh, it wasn't an injury," she said. "It was a disease. Freddy should never have been playing at all. He had bad legs, a hereditary problem. His father died from complications brought on by the same disease. That was what took Freddy out of baseball. The disease was also why he went away — you've been kind not to pry — but I don't have any animosity. He went away because he loved me very much."

"That's a little hard to understand," I said. "Did you have a family?"

"No. Oh, we'd planned to have a baby, the very summer Freddy took ill. He'd never supposed his father's illness to be hereditary. But after he found out, Freddy didn't want to bring any children into the world. I couldn't talk him out of it.

" 'You make a life for yourself, Mary,' he said. His leaving broke both our hearts. Freddy was so proud. You only had to watch him on the bases to see how proud he was of his ability. He couldn't stand the thought of losing those abilities and he couldn't stand the thought of me seeing him lose his abilities." She paused and smiled her slow, sad smile. "But I've stayed with him anyway," she said.

"Do you have a good photograph?" I asked. "The newspaper photos I've seen were poor quality, and it seems to me the baseball cards in those days managed to make all the players look alike."

The photos I'd seen of Freddy Schiraldi showed a thin, dark-complexioned young man with deep-set eyes.

"The one you'd probably like to see is the one he sent after he left me. I only heard from him once. About a year after he left he sent me a note and a photograph from Mobile, Alabama."

She went into her bedroom and returned with a chocolate box full of photographs. She produced a black-and-white, wallet-sized photo, one with a scalloped edge, showing Freddy standing behind the counter of a tiny restaurant, likely a converted boxcar. The photograph was of a small, sad man with blue cheeks and short hair, wearing a white shirt with the sleeves rolled up and a dirty apron.

" 'I'm doing okay,' the letter said. 'Coaching a little baseball, earning my keep. I love you.' And that was all. I never heard from him again."

"What can you tell me that was unusual?" I said. "Something unique about Freddy, peculiar, humorous?"

Mary Schiraldi smiled a sweet smile, overflowing with memories. "Freddy never went to a barber in his life. His mother cut his hair with a pair of hand clippers that she oiled with 3-in-One Oil before every clipping. When we got married he brought the clippers with him and I cut his hair, just clipped up the sides and back with the clippers, trimmed off the top with scissors. When he went away he took the clippers and scissors with him. And, of course, he had a tic at the corner of his left eye. It danced even when he was asleep. If you look closely at the photograph you can see it."

"Do you think he's still alive?"

"Oh, no. When Freddy left me he went away to die. He said he wanted to teach a few boys the art of base stealing before he passed on. I hope he did."

Four years have gone by since my interview with Mary Schiraldi. She passed away about five months ago. I received a letter containing the picture of Freddy behind the lunch counter, along with a brief note from Mrs. Schiraldi's younger sister saying she found it in an envelope addressed to me in the chocolate box. I studied the photo. I thought I could see the corner of his eye twitching.

I did the story on the base stealers, in fact I've done at least two a year each year since. I mentioned Sweet Freddy Schiraldi, told what I knew of him, disclosed how he was one of the big leaguers who had slipped through the cracks of time and asked any readers who knew anything about him to write to me in care of *Sports Center Magazine*.

I received 105 replies. I suppose I should have expected that many. *Sports Center* has a circulation of over a million, which means roughly five million readers. Most of the replies were reminiscences by people who had seen and appreciated the play of Sweet Freddy Schiraldi.

One of his teammates from the Browns wrote to tell me about Freddy's special shoe. When he was a boy Freddy complained to his father that he couldn't get good enough footing for a fast start on a steal, so his father the shoemaker made him a special cleat, longer than the others by half an inch, that Freddy used to gouge out starting blocks for his feet on minor-league base paths, and later in the American League ballparks.

I took the four or five most promising letters to my editor, and asked for time and money to follow them up.

"So what are you gonna do if you find him?" he asked, then without waiting for a reply went on. "He's likely been dead for years; these leads don't look wonderful. No point in us doing research for Cooperstown and *The Baseball Encyclopedia*. You mentioned him in your article, got a reaction, let's move on to some new angle. Speaking of which, have any of these base stealers run against a racehorse recently? Maybe we could set it up."

I decided to follow up the leads with my own time and money.

"If base stealing had been regarded as important in the thirties," an ex–New York Yankee wrote to me, "Freddy Schiraldi could have stolen a couple of hundred bases a season. He swiveled like a running back when he stole, ran low to the ground, slid like a rush of water. I met a fellow who knew someone who had a relative who saw Freddy down in Mississippi somewhere in the late forties. He was teaching little black boys how not to get caught stealing bases."

As my investigation continued, a pattern slowly emerged. It seemed that just as Freddy sent only one letter to his wife after he left Jersey City, he always reported back to one person after he changed locations. Among the replies that the magazine article brought me was a letter from a woman in Mobile, Alabama. She had been a waitress at the diner where Freddy, perched on a kitchen stool because of his bad leg, worked as a short-order cook.

"He showed me his leg once," she wrote. "It was horrible, all blue and swollen, covered with scabs and scars. He coached a team at a boys club in the neighborhood. One of the boys told me Freddy would demonstrate a feet-first slide, then come up white with pain, the effort hurt his leg so much.

"About a year after he left Mobile he wrote me from a little town in Nebraska. Said he was real excited about a ten-year-old boy named Whitey, swore that boy was going to be a star. I don't follow baseball enough to know if he did or not, and I never heard from Freddy Schiraldi again."

It hardly seemed a coincidence that Richie "Whitey" Ashburn led the National League in stolen bases in his rookie year of 1948. He would have been ten years old in 1937 and was living in or near Tilden, Nebraska.

Tilden, Nebraska, is one of a string of small towns on Highway 275, none of them near any major city. It wasn't hard to find an old-timer who remembered Freddy Schiraldi.

"Gimpy Freddy is what we called him. Skinny little guy with a real bad leg. Walked with a terrible limp. Worked at a café on the highway and helped out with the school baseball team. I don't remember that he coached Richie Ashburn personally. Hell, everybody within a hundred-mile radius liked to claim they was the one first spotted that boy as a big leaguer. What became of Freddy?

Haven't a clue. But I did hear that the principal of the school heard from him a few years after he left here. Was in California somewhere, claimed to have a hot baseball prospect."

That was the pattern. Sweet Freddy Schiraldi moved inconspicuously across the face of America sniffing out the base stealers of the future, recognizing them before anyone else did, giving them a gentle push, like a wind at their backs. A kindly, shy, lonely man, he asked for nothing but the pleasure of dispensing his knowledge of baseball. As I followed his route, crossing and recrossing America, I was amazed to see that he at least briefly touched the lives of almost every major base stealer of the past forty years. Some barely remembered him because they had only a single lesson, delivered from a wheelchair by a small, emaciated man who never once mentioned his own big-league career.

Somewhere in his travels he lost or dispensed with his last name and one of his legs. He was remembered as Gimpy Freddy, One-Legged Freddy, the guy in the wheelchair, the old man. Along the way he crossed the paths of Maury Wills, Lou Brock, Rickey Henderson, Tim Raines, Ron LeFlore, Freddie Patek, Davey Lopes, Joe Morgan, Bert Campaneris, and dozens of other baseball greats who made base stealing a part of their careers.

In my search, I was always ten years or more behind him. For by the time I would find a young man who had been tutored by Sweet Freddy Schiraldi and had reached the major leagues at age twenty-two to twenty-five, it was ten or twelve years since he'd seen Freddy. I would find that Freddy had taught someone in a small southern town the crossover step. "Think football," he told him. Or that he had found someone who, like him, thought of base stealing as track and dug him his first footholds, recommending that he install a long cleat on his shoe.

"The jump is what is important, not the lead," he told another. "Read the pitcher. You steal off the pitcher, not the catcher." A one-legged old man in a wheelchair cannot demonstrate the down-and-up slide, accelerating hard into the bag at second, but Freddy Schiraldi could talk a good game. He would watch these boys slide, give directions. "Now, now," he would shout, "down hard, but up and ready to run. Always be ready to take that extra base."

"You've got to have a perfect body to be a great thief," he would say. "Base-stealing takes a terrible toll: jammed shoulders, dislocated fingers, twisted and sprained ankles, your back, your neck . . ."

Freddy had long outlived his life expectancy. I kept hearing of him; he seemed to drop from the sky, an old man with a magic wand he touched to the bodies of young base runners, who were suddenly able to dart like dragonflies from base to base, to scorch the earth with their speed, leave their shadows at first while they fled to second almost undetected.

"He was so thin he might have been made of paper," a woman in rural Georgia, from whom he had rented a room, told me. "He got thinner while he was here with me, though, Lord knows, I tried my best to fatten him up a little."

"Oh, but he could smell a good baseball player," a restaurant owner in Kentucky told me. " 'Are you a scout?' I asked him. 'Sort of an independent,' he replied. 'But I'm more of a teacher than a scout.'

"He came into my café and offered to wash dishes for meals and a few dollars, said he was aiming to watch a local boy play ball, young fellow no more than thirteen. Nobody'd spotted him as a star. But he became one locally after he'd worked with Freddy, and he's in Triple A now waiting for the call to the Bigs.

" 'How did you know about that young fella?' I asked Freddy. 'How did you know to come here and teach him to run?'

" 'I have a nose for fast-running ballplayers,' he said. 'I smell them out, the way a bear finds honey. I'm searching for the perfect base stealer,' he went on.

" 'How will you know when you find him?' I asked.

" 'I'll know because I won't have to search anymore,' said Freddy."

I decided I was never going to catch up with Freddy Schiraldi without help. Over the years one of my best friends in baseball has been Bill Clark, head scout for the Cincinnati Reds. He wrote to me once to tell me how much he enjoyed a piece I'd written for *Sports Center;* I wrote back; we became friends. I called him at his home in Columbia, Missouri.

"What do you know about Freddy Schiraldi?" I asked.

"Phantom Freddy," said Bill. "I'm not sure he really exists. I meet boys who claim they spent a day or a week or even several months being tutored by this guy Freddy, an old man with one leg, who travels around the country in a motorized wheelchair. I guess he exists, or a lot of young ballplayers have had the same delusion. But our paths have never crossed. He gets to players before we do, always."

Bill is an infinitely patient man. He crisscrosses America in an endless search for baseball talent. He is a bird watcher who has learned to drive in the slow lane of the interstates, reading a book as he travels from ballpark to ballpark.

"Keep your eyes and ears open for me, will you? I hear Sweet Freddy is fading away, literally as well as physically. I want to interview him once before he dies."

"If I hear anything, you'll be the first to know," said Bill Clark.

And I know I was. Still, it was nearly two years before he called me at *Sports Center.*

"I got a hot tip yesterday," Bill said. "Do you know where Natchitoches, Louisiana, is?"

"Up in the boonies north of Baton Rouge somewhere?"

"Guy who keeps his eyes open for me said he saw a young boy, name of Foreshaw, no more than fourteen, who runs like he was shot out of a cannon, has more raw talent than he's ever seen in one body. My friend says he's a singles hitter who steals second and third like they were his private property. But the most interesting thing he said was that the boy has an extra-long cleat on one shoe, that he uses to dig starting blocks."

Natchitoches (pronounced *Naka-dish*) is a university town in northwest Louisiana, 75 miles south of Shreveport, 150 miles north of Baton Rouge, which means it is a long way from *anywhere.*

I took a week of holidays, flew to Shreveport, rented a car, and drove to Natchitoches. I started by canvassing the few downtown restaurants. In small southern towns everyone knows everyone else's business.

"There was an old man in a wheelchair worked down the street at Lasyones since last fall, but he's gone now, just up and disappeared not even a week ago."

Lasyones was a down-home Creole restaurant where I ate red beans and rice with spiced sausage. When I finished my meal I asked the waitress about Freddy.

"Gone," she said. "But he was a friend of Lolly the cook."

A moment later a very large black woman, wrapped in yards of white apron and wearing a squashed white chef's cap, lumbered from the kitchen to my table.

"Strange thing is he left his wheelchair behind," she said. "Lordy, but there was nothin' to that man but his clothes. He closed the place up at night. I found it locked up tight when I come to work of a mornin' last week, but his chair was inside. He couldn't get but from his chair to a bed, stayed with a friend over in our part of town. Left his clothes and shaving gear at her house. You the law?"

"No, ma'am, I'm a baseball fan. I heard Freddy was the best base-stealing coach around."

"An' it's my boy he's been teachin'," she said, smiling. "He said Estes was a sure thing to make the big time. 'He's the best I've ever seen, Lolly,' poor old Freddy said to me. I wish he could have stayed around to help the boy on his way. Poor black boy from this backwater, need somebody to steer him right."

"I'd like to watch your son play," I said.

"Try tonight," she replied, and gave me directions to the ballfield on the far side of town. "Sure don't git it from my side of the house, but that boy can run like a turpentined cat. Oh, and there's something else, something that worries me. My boy's taken to screwin' up his face 'til he resemble that old man. What do you think of that?"

The divisions run deep this far south. At the game, I was the only white face in the crowd.

His first time up Estes Foreshaw walked on five pitches. He loped off to first swiveling his hips and shoulders as if he had fresh oil in all his joints. He wore a pair of ragged white uniform pants and a blue T-shirt. At first he pawed the earth with the one long cleat on his baseball shoes. He dug like a dog intending to hide something. He aimed himself toward second, his feet braced in the starting blocks he had created. The interesting thing was that his lead was very short; he was not far enough off first to even draw a throw. He stole on the second pitch, his run like a time-lapse photograph, one eighty-seven-foot-long white-and-blue blur. The catcher did not throw. The shortstop was still five feet from the bag when Estes arrived, sliding hard, coming up ready to run in case of an overthrow.

He scored on a single up the middle, whooshed across the plate, slapped hands with his teammates, and returned to the bench.

"Way to run, Estes," one of the boys called.

"Squirted round them bases like you was greased," cried another.

I moved over and sat beside him. He glared at me suspiciously, his shoulders in an insolent slump. I stared him straight in the eye; he half grinned at me, embarrassed. The Schiraldi tic wiggled like an insect in the corner of his left eye.

I smiled at the boy, Estes Foreshaw, the next phenomenal base stealer in whichever major league he winds up, perhaps the greatest base stealer of all time. The boy is built solid as a grain sack, yet flexible as rope.

"You're gonna steal fifteen hundred in the Bigs," I said to him, playfully removing his cap.

"You think so?" he said, for an instant almost trusting me. But the suspicion returned to his eyes as I reached out and tapped him on the forehead, lightly, like knocking on a thin door.

"Freddy?" I said. "Freddy, are you in there?"